CHASING

VENGEANCE

REDEMPTION HARBOR SERIES

Katie Reus

Cover art: Jaycee of Sweet 'N Spicy Designs
Editor: Julia Ganis
Author website: https://www.katiereus.com

Publisher's Note: This is a work of fiction. Names, characters, places, and
incidents are either the products of the author's imagination or used ficti-
tiously, and any resemblance to actual persons, living or dead, or business
establishments, organizations or locales is completely coincidental.

Chasing Vengeance /Katie Reus. -- 1st ed.
KR Press, LLC

ISBN-13: 978-1-63556-098-5
ISBN-10: 1-63556-098-5

eISBN: 9781635560978

For Kaylea Cross. Thank you for our plotting trip to New Orleans and for always being there. You are the best!

Praise for the novels of Katie Reus

"Exciting in more ways than one, well-paced and smoothly written, I'd recommend *A Covert Affair* to any romantic suspense reader."
—Harlequin Junkie

"Sexy military romantic suspense." —USA Today

"I could not put this book down. . . . Let me be clear that I am not saying that this was a good book *for* a paranormal genre; it was an excellent romance read, *period.*" —All About Romance

"Reus strikes just the right balance of steamy sexual tension and nail-biting action....This romantic thriller reliably hits every note that fans of the genre will expect." —*Publishers Weekly*

"Prepare yourself for the start of a great new series! . . . I'm excited about reading more about this great group of characters."
—Fresh Fiction

"Wow! This powerful, passionate hero sizzles with sheer deliciousness. I loved every sexy twist of this fun & exhilarating tale. Katie Reus delivers!" —Carolyn Crane, RITA award winning author

"A sexy, well-crafted paranormal romance that succeeds with smart characters and creative world building."—Kirkus Reviews

"*Mating Instinct*'s romance is taut and passionate . . . Katie Reus's newest installment in her Moon Shifter series will leave readers breathless!"
—Stephanie Tyler, *New York Times* bestselling author

"You'll fall in love with Katie's heroes."
—*New York Times* bestselling author, Kaylea Cross

"Both romantic and suspenseful, a fast-paced sexy book full of high stakes action." —Heroes and Heartbreakers

"Katie Reus pulls the reader into a story line of second chances, betrayal, and the truth about forgotten lives and hidden pasts."
—The Reading Café

"Nonstop action, a solid plot, good pacing, and riveting suspense."
—RT Book Reviews

"Enough sexual tension to set the pages on fire."
—*New York Times* bestselling author, Alexandra Ivy

"...a wild hot ride for readers. The story grabs you and doesn't let go."
—*New York Times* bestselling author, Cynthia Eden

"Has all the right ingredients: a hot couple, evil villains, and a killer action-filled plot. . . . [The] Moon Shifter series is what I call Grade-A entertainment!" —Joyfully Reviewed

"*Avenger's Heat* hits the ground running...This is a story of strength, of partnership and healing, and it does it brilliantly."
—Vampire Book Club

"*Mating Instinct* was a great read with complex characters, serious political issues and a world I am looking forward to coming back to."
—All Things Urban Fantasy

CHAPTER ONE

—My book club only reads wine labels.—

Layla inhaled the crisp, cold air as she stepped out onto the sidewalk from the café she'd just been in with Skye and some of their friends. The others were staying a little bit longer but she and Skye were headed out.

"So who texted you earlier that got you blushing?" Skye asked in that abrupt, no-nonsense way of hers.

"I have no idea what you're talking about," Layla said, glancing across the street where her little car was parked. She really needed to get new tires this week. And probably get her oil changed.

"Liar, liar, pants on fire. Come on, are you dating again?"

"I kind of can't believe you're even asking me." Normally the only things Skye wanted to talk about were self-defense classes and weapons and stuff Layla generally had no interest in or even understood. It was a miracle she'd convinced Skye to join this book club because she really did adore the woman. And Skye had been a good friend to her after everything that happened to Layla last year—including helping to save her life. Literally.

"I can't believe I'm asking either. Colt thinks I'm 'growing.' His words, not mine." She snorted.

Layla grinned. "Fine. No, I'm not dating, and I wasn't blushing. You are most definitely mistaken."

Skye frowned slightly. "Do you smell that?"

Layla glanced around. The scent of coffee filled the air, combined with normal street smells. Though the street was mostly deserted, probably because it was freezing outside. Everyone was inside, drinking hot cocoa or wine or whatever and bundled up where it was warm.

"It's your pants. They're on fire."

Despite herself, Layla giggled at Skye's deadpan expression. "Holy cats, you're ridiculous. Fine, Xavier texted me to let me know he was back in town." She'd met him a few months ago at a friend's rehearsal dinner, and while she was attracted to him, it was very clear he was only interested in friendship.

Which was just as well. She was getting her life back together after the insanity of last year when she discovered that her fiancé was a monster who ran drugs, weapons, and people. When she'd witnessed him murder an undercover DEA agent, she'd turned to her best friend Nova, who in turn had recruited all her friends who owned Redemption Harbor Consulting. Layla had even gone into witness protection for a couple weeks before it was clear that her now dead fiancé would no longer be a problem for her.

Skye's expression darkened ever so slightly. If Layla hadn't been looking at her friend, she might have missed it. "What?" Layla asked.

Skye lifted a shoulder and pulled out her key fob. "Nothing. But he's dangerous."

"To me?" Layla stilled as she asked the question, her heart rate kicking up a notch. She trusted Skye's opinion. More than her own at this point, considering her track record with men. The woman was a badass and trained in all sorts of martial arts, and though Layla wasn't quite sure what she'd done for a living before founding a "consulting company," she knew it was government related. Most likely CIA, just as Nova had been. Though she didn't think Skye had been an analyst. She had too much of an edge about her to be suited to a desk job. And she'd once heard Nova say in an offhand way that Skye carried around explosives—and she didn't think her best friend had been joking. Not to mention Skye's little dog was literally named C-4.

"Definitely not. He'd be dead if he was." There was no humor in Skye's voice, which made Layla blink.

She shook off the statement though, because she was getting used to some of the random things her friend said. "Then what do you mean? He's in finance and investing." He certainly traveled enough for that to be true and she had no reason not to believe him. He was friends with Axel, after all, and Axel worked for Redemption Harbor Consulting. She wasn't totally clear on what they all did, but they helped people for a living. They literally helped people in need get out of serious jams. She didn't think they'd be friends with anyone who was like her ex. Scratch that, she knew they wouldn't.

Skye simply snorted and pressed the unlock button on the truck she was driving. Layla often saw her in different vehicles and she wasn't sure what Skye actually owned. According to Skye, the ones she drove were all company-owned, so it could be anything.

"What's that supposed to mean?"

Skye lifted a shoulder. "Are you sleeping with him or are you planning to sleep with him?"

"Skye!"

Skye just raised her eyebrows. Her long auburn hair was pulled back into a tight braid tonight, which was more or less her signature style. Though Layla had a feeling it had more to do with efficiency than actual style.

Layla stared right back but lost the staring contest. As usual. "No. We're just friends. Seriously." She wasn't going to admit how attracted to Xavier she was because clearly her taste in the opposite sex was complete and utter garbage. She should learn her lesson after what she'd been through.

"Good, then. Stay friends with him and nothing more."

"You want to expand any on that?"

"Look, he's not a danger to you *at all*. But...he's not a safe and cuddly teacher either."

"Teachers are...cuddly?"

She threw her hands up. "Whatever. You're a teacher and you're so sweet. I was just giving an example, but that's probably the wrong word. I meant he's nothing like you." Skye pulled her into a hug. "I've got to get home. I have a sexy man waiting for me in bed. Plus I miss C-4. Are you okay to drive?"

She nodded once, not bothering to pull on the Xavier thread any longer. Layla had learned that when Skye was done talking about something, she was done and nothing would change it. "Yeah, I only had that one glass of wine and that was over an hour ago." Not that she actually planned to drive home anytime soon but she wasn't going to tell Skye that.

As they spoke, a familiar SUV pulled up across the street and parked behind her little car. Damn it. Layla had left out the little fact that Xavier would be meeting her after book club so they could head down the street and grab a bite to eat.

Next to her Skye tensed but Layla put a gentle hand on her forearm. "It's just Xavier. We're going to grab drinks and food."

Skye shot her a sideways glance. "How is this not a date?"

She nudged her friend once with her hip. "Hush."

Instead of leaving, Skye waited until Xavier got out and crossed the street.

Xavier's dark hair was cut short—and showed off those ridiculous cheekbones. He was broad-shouldered and, according to her best friend Nova, "scary looking," but Layla didn't see it. Yes, he was huge and muscular and had multiple scars, including a pale one on the right side of his face that had faded with age, but his dark green eyes were soft when they looked at her.

She'd been engaged to a ridiculously handsome, charming man who'd been a monster underneath. He'd done and said all the right things, and looking back, she wondered if she hadn't seen the red flags because he "looked safe." Xavier...okay, he looked like a lethal predator, but she *felt* safe around him. With her ex, she'd felt like he was a safe choice, but not necessarily that she was safe around him. And after a while, she'd simply been terrified of him.

Skye didn't smile as Xavier approached, but Layla gave him a big hug. He was strong and solid against her. She was sorely tempted to bury her face against his neck and inhale his masculine scent. But since she wasn't crazy, she resisted the urge. "I'm glad you came back early," she said, meaning it. He traveled a lot, mostly overseas, and they kept in touch via FaceTime and texting. But she still liked seeing him in person.

She decided to ignore the sensation of butterflies taking flight inside her as he hugged her back, squeezing tight.

Once he let go of her, he nodded politely at Skye, who gave him a neutral smile. "Xavier," she said mildly.

"Skye, you're looking well," he said, his tone just as neutral.

Skye paused before glancing between the two of them. "She better make it home safe tonight," she said before giving Layla another quick hug, then left.

Once her friend was gone, Layla shook her head slightly. "I think she views me as a little sister. She gets kind of protective."

Xavier shrugged as they started walking down the sidewalk. "I'm glad. It's good to have people to look out for you."

"Who looks out for you?" she asked before she could think about censoring herself.

He glanced down at her, surprise in his expression. "No one looks out for me. I'm the Big Bad Wolf." His lips kicked up at the corners as if he was fighting a laugh.

She snorted at that and laid her head on his shoulder. She really had missed him. When he started dating someone, she'd have to pull back from their friendship because it would hurt too much to see him with another woman, but she enjoyed spending time with him. He had a dry humor she appreciated, and more than that, kind eyes.

Despite what Skye said about him being dangerous, something about him made her feel safe. Of course her judgment was all sorts of screwed up so maybe she was wrong about him too. But...she didn't think so.

Right now it felt like she was learning to do things again. Making new friends, trying to figure out if she still wanted to teach full-time, where the heck she wanted to live. Her life wasn't a mess, exactly, but she felt very un-tethered to the world right now. Being with Xavier seemed to somehow anchor her and she appreciated that. "So I guess you finished up your investment stuff early, huh?" Well, duh, she internally chided herself. He wouldn't be back unless he'd finished. But she rambled when she got nervous and asked obvious questions. *Gah.*

"I finished up work early, yes." He gave her a small grin as he continued. "And I couldn't wait to get back to you."

"Ha, ha." She nudged him once, wishing his words were true. Sometimes he low-level flirted with her, but he'd never made a move or insinuated he wanted anything more.

And yes, she could make a move, but that wasn't her style. She wasn't bold enough, and even if she had been, after her ex, she was gun-shy when it came to, well, everything. If Xavier made a move, however, that might change things.

* * *

Xavier wanted to smack the little shit who was shamelessly flirting with Layla.

Their waiter had been staring at her from the moment he'd walked up to their outdoor table and introduced himself. It wasn't like Xavier could blame the guy—she was adorable, beautiful...perfect. Usually he couldn't take his eyes off her either. This little shit was lucky that Xavier had self-control. For now.

"So, red or white?" the man with the GQ looks asked, completely ignoring Xavier as he stared at Layla as if she hung the moon.

"Well, I had red earlier so I'll stick with it for tonight." Layla's voice was soft and sweet. She'd left her dark hair down tonight so that it cascaded around her shoulders and breasts, and he wanted nothing more than to run his fingers through it, to see how soft it was. He was surprised she'd wanted to sit outside, but there were heaters and so far the cold didn't seem to be bothering her.

"If you're not sure what you want, I can give you a few free samples," the waiter continued, lowering his voice as if telling her a secret.

"That sounds great," she said, smiling up at the guy.

The insane part of Xavier wanted her smiles all to himself. When she looked at him, that full, wide-open smile still in place, he felt it like a punch to his chest.

"What about you?" she asked.

"Water is fine," he said, staring at their server, his expression probably as dark as he felt now.

The guy practically ran away from their table but Xavier didn't care. He knew the way he felt about her was possessive. Even if he had no right to feel possessive over her.

He'd never expected to meet someone like her. He'd never expected Layla, period. But she was in his life now even if they were destined to be friends only. He'd take what he could get. He knew a little bit about what she'd been through last year—that her ex-fiancé was dead, and she'd seen him murder someone—and though he wanted to push for more details, it had clearly upset her so he'd held off. He could look it up on his own, but somehow that had felt wrong, like he was checking up on her. In the past, something like that never would have bothered him, but he hadn't wanted to violate her trust.

There was no way she was ready for a new relationship regardless. Not that it mattered. He didn't do relationships anyway. Sex was all he was capable of.

But Layla deserved more than that, and he was no good for her anyway. His hands were too bloodstained. She deserved someone a hell of a lot better than a man who killed for a living. Not only that, if they got involved romantically, it would paint a target on her back. They were just friends. Plain and simple.

Though nothing about his feelings for her were plain or simple.

"I think you scared off our waiter," she said, laughing lightly. She wrapped her arms around herself even though they were sitting underneath the heater. She'd wanted to sit outside instead of inside and he hadn't cared one way or the other. Whatever she wanted, she got.

The fitted black jacket she wore over her sweater and tight jeans didn't do much to hide those luscious curves. He wished he had the right to touch and caress her everywhere. To run his fingers through her hair, to hold the back of her head tight as he dominated her mouth, to look into her amber eyes as she rode him. *Fuck. Nope.* Had to shut that thought down right now.

He cleared his throat. "I didn't like the way he was flirting with you." It wasn't as if they were on a date, but that guy didn't know that. "For all he knows, we're together."

She laughed again, that melodic sound driving him crazy. "You're ridiculous. He's simply doing his job. He probably thinks that if he flirts, he'll get a better tip."

He resisted the urge to snort. The guy was giving her free samples and Xavier had been here enough times with her to know they didn't do free samples. Instead he simply lifted a shoulder. "So how was book club?"

"It was good. I got to see my girls—and talk about books while drinking wine. I call that a good Friday night. And I feel like I'm settling in a little more here." There was a note in her voice he couldn't quite place. "Did you stop in Orlando before heading back here?" she asked before he could respond.

"No, not this time." He probably should have, because he missed his family, but he'd cut his trip short as soon as he finished his contract because he'd been desperate to see Layla. Which, again, was stupid on his part. But he couldn't stop his obsession with her. He wasn't sure he wanted to. Even though it was destined to end badly.

When his friend Axel had invited him to a wedding last year, he couldn't believe Axel was getting married. Men like them didn't do marriages and relationships. But Axel had quit his former job as a hit man and now was...happy.

When Xavier met Axel's wife, Hadley, he'd understood why his friend was settling down. And then he'd met Layla...and he'd started to wonder if maybe he could have the same thing.

He mentally shut down that thought too. He was already fighting a hard on by simply being in the same vicinity as her.

"I'm sure your grandmother is disappointed," Layla said, shaking her head slightly.

He was sure of that too. "I'll see her soon."

"Tell me about your recent trip," she said even as their server brought her little samples of wine, a charming smile on his face.

The man started telling her which kind was which and making suggestions, so Xavier sat back and was silent as the man went through his little spiel.

Layla ended up choosing a glass of Beaujolais and he ordered an appetizer for them. He'd eaten on the plane, but it hadn't been much and he was starving. Though he was starving for a hell of a lot more than food.

When Layla turned to him after their server left, giving him that wide smile, he experienced that same strange sensation in his chest again. *Damn, that smile should be illegal.*

He really needed to lock down his feelings for her. He'd been compartmentalizing shit his entire life. From the day his parents had died.

But when he was around Layla, it was as if the lid to his control just popped off and he struggled to keep himself contained.

Struggled to keep his feelings for her shut down. Because maybe he didn't want to anymore. And wasn't that a kick in the ass.

CHAPTER TWO

—You bring the wine, I'll bring the bad decisions.—

"Thanks for driving me home," Layla said, settling against Xavier's warm leather seat. His SUV was the most comfortable vehicle she'd ever been in. The upholstery was butter smooth and she loved the seat warmers. But really, she loved the company more than anything.

"No problem. I can pick you up tomorrow and take you back to get your car." His deep voice rumbled in the interior, wrapping around her, making her wish that maybe things were different between them.

That just maybe they were more than friends... *Nope.* No, no, no. Just no. Not going there. Because then her mind started to wander, to fantasize. And that was doing no one any good, least of all her.

"You don't have to do that. I can call a car service or something." She probably would've been fine to drive home after the wine but it wasn't worth the risk. She'd had enough drama to last a lifetime. She wasn't going to be irresponsible on top of everything. "How long are you going to be in town this time?"

"I'm not sure."

Yep, that was definite disappointment that rolled through her at his words. He traveled a lot and she was always sad to see him go. More than once she'd wondered if he was sleeping with other women during his trips, but she shut that thought down. It wasn't her business. They weren't together; they weren't anything other than friends. Even if she sometimes fantasized otherwise. Okay, more than sometimes.

"I need to do some shopping tomorrow, grab a few things for my place." The last he'd told her, he was basically living out of boxes. He'd moved here not long after Axel's wedding and she still hadn't seen his place. "Would you want to come with me?" he continued.

"Of course," she said, not exactly surprised he'd asked her. It wouldn't be the first shopping trip they'd gone on. Usually they just went to new restaurants, plays or movies, but he'd asked for her advice on clothing before. Making him even more adorable. "I'm kind of curious to see where you live anyway."

He grinned at her as he pulled into her driveway. "I think you're going to be very disappointed when you see it. I've got a bed, a couch, and a TV."

She wondered what kind of bed it was. It would be big. Big enough for him and some lucky woman to... *Ugh. No.* Thinking of him with another woman made her all but choke with jealousy. "Let me guess, it's a big-screen TV?"

He lifted a shoulder, that sexy-as-sin grin of his still in place.

"Guys are so predictable."

He laughed lightly as he got out. He'd rounded the front of the vehicle before she'd even unstrapped. Even with the heat running, she was still chilled to her finger-tips. She blamed it on her Puerto Rican heritage. Her body preferred sun and sand, not snow. Though she really did love the changing of the seasons. And right now South Carolina was like a winter wonderland. Thankfully there wasn't much snow on the ground. Just a dusting of it covering everything, making everything feel light and magical. As if anything could happen.

He took her hand as he helped her get out. And even though she didn't need help at all, she gladly took his hand in hers. She still liked touching him even if they both had gloves on. As usual, she had to ignore that little jolt of electricity she experienced. When she slid out onto her feet, he looked down at her with the most heated expression. It was so intense her breath caught in her throat, and though it was impossible, it felt as if her heart skipped a beat. She'd never seen him look at her like that before, with such raw hunger. But...maybe she was mistaken?

Before she could dissect that look, he turned away and shut the door behind her. Just like that, the moment dissipated like smoke and she started to question herself. Maybe she had drunk too much wine.

"Come on," he said abruptly, his voice rough, "let's get you inside. It's cold."

It might be cold but she suddenly felt flushed. "Do you want to come inside for a few minutes?" she blurted out, then inwardly winced. He'd come in before but for some reason her words sounded like an invitation this time.

Maybe they were. Maybe the wine really had gone to her head tonight.

As they reached the top of the few steps to her porch, he took her keys from her hands and unlocked the door for her. She was glad because her fingers were numb as a weird anticipation settled in her bones. "I think I'll take a rain check," he said quietly. "What time did you want me to pick you up tomorrow?"

His hot-and-cold routine was jarring. Confusing as hell. Even if she wanted to pretend she'd misread that look, she was almost certain she hadn't. "Early is fine for me. I'm sure you want to get an early start." He could just do online shopping but she was glad he wanted to go to physical shops tomorrow because she would get to spend time with him.

He stepped closer, invading her personal space for a long moment as he brushed a few wayward strands of hair out of her face. Her heart skipped a beat then went into frantic double time as she stared up at him.

On instinct she leaned into his hand, then froze as he stared down at her.

His gaze dropped to her lips and there it was again, that raw hunger that said he wanted to devour her mouth as he pinned her up against her front door. Or maybe the door-pinning was just wishful thinking on her part.

She clenched her thighs together at that thought. Something told her that sex with him would be wild and rough and she would enjoy every second of it. Her nipples beaded tightly against her bra as they stood there staring at each other. Her breath curled in front of her in little wisps of white as time stood still.

For a moment, he started to lean down, as if he was going to kiss her. She stepped forward, placing her hands on his chest and leaning up on tiptoe, but he froze. Then pulled back so abruptly she might have stumbled as he put a few inches between them.

Oh God. Embarrassment burned her cheeks as she stepped back and toward her door. Right about now it would be awesome if the ground would open up and swallow her. "Thanks again," she muttered, grabbing her key out of the door as she shoved it open. She felt kind of rude for hurrying inside so quickly, but she wasn't sure what had just happened.

Okay that was a lie, she was pretty sure she'd been about to jump him but he'd pulled back as if she'd set him on fire. Or stabbed him. *Ugh.*

She could analyze why he'd pulled back a hundred different ways, but in the end it didn't matter. Because he had. Because he didn't want to kiss her. Because they were just friends.

And she was a total dumbass. She let her head fall back against her front door even as she locked it behind her. She was definitely going to file this under "things I wish I could forget." She'd let her wishful thinking get away from her. She'd thought he'd been looking at her differently tonight but nope, she'd probably had more wine than she realized.

Awesome.

* * *

Xavier winced as Layla's lock clicked into place. Damn, he'd screwed that up good. But he hadn't been prepared for that wild spark of heat that had arced between them so sharp and fierce it had been like a physical thing. He'd been attracted to her from the moment he'd met her. And yes, he'd gotten flashes of interest from her too, but it had always been subdued. Nothing like what had just happened.

Right now, he felt as if he'd been run over by a truck. And nothing had even happened.

"Layla?" he called out.

"Yeah?" she said, clearly still standing by the front door.

"Make sure you set your alarm." He couldn't help it. He had this innate need to keep her safe. And keeping her safe meant staying the hell away from her no matter what he wanted.

He heard the little beep of her security system arming, and since this was Nova's home—that Layla was staying in temporarily—he knew for a fact that her fiancé had installed a state-of-the-art system. Even Xavier couldn't hack it. Of course if someone wanted to get inside, they would just smash a window or kick down the door, but at least there was a system in place to warn Layla of any trouble.

Cursing himself, he headed back to his SUV—which had tinted, bullet-resistant windows and tires resistant to punctures. Because you never knew when you were going to be in a high-speed chase, and he didn't like taking chances with his safety. He also had a few other measures in place for those "just in case" things that might happen. Things like armed attacks.

As he reached the front door of his vehicle, a little tingling started in the back of his neck. The one that told him someone was watching him.

Sliding into the front seat, he didn't start the engine. Instead, he glanced around Layla's neighborhood. Across the street, he saw some movement behind one of the front windows. If a nosy neighbor was spying on Layla, they were doing a poor job of it. The person's body was lit up by the interior lights, so he could clearly see the curtains moving to the side. So either it was a nosy neighbor setting off his alarm bells, or someone was watching him with other intents. Layla had told him she had a few curious neighbors, which wasn't exactly a bad thing. Because people like that had their place—they were the ones who called the cops when worried about shit.

Still, he sat in her driveway, waiting, because he didn't like that feeling at the back of his neck. He'd escaped death far too many times to ignore his intuition. Of course, right now his head was all fucked up. Because he'd stopped what would have likely been an incredible kiss. And who was he kidding? If he'd kissed her, he wouldn't have stopped.

Because he didn't think she'd wanted to either. He would have had her naked and his face buried between her legs before they'd even hit the stairs. He'd have made her come twice before thrusting inside her.

"Fuck," he muttered to himself, starting the engine. He let the warmth fill the interior but he kept the exterior and interior lights off.

He was always careful on jobs and he only took contract work where nothing was personal. Personal stuff got you killed. His jobs were all about survival and making money.

That didn't mean he didn't have enemies. Still, he couldn't think of anyone who wanted to target him right now. But he sat and waited for roughly half an hour until that feeling went away. Only then did he head home, but he called Gage on the way.

"What's up?" the hacker asked.

"I know you have a good security system installed in Nova's house," he said, not bothering with any sort of niceties. What was the point? He'd met the other man through Axel. And he liked Gage, liked his reputation. That didn't mean they were friends. Just friendly enough. "Do you have any other security system around the perimeter of her place? Like cameras?"

"Yeah. Why?"

"I don't know. I dropped Layla off tonight and had a weird feeling. Probably nothing." Or more likely it was just the remnants of his last job hanging on, combined with what had almost happened between him and Layla tonight. But he still wanted to keep an eye on her place.

"I've got cameras set up, but I don't actively monitor them now."

"Can you send me the login to the cameras?" He wasn't sure what type of system Gage had set up but it stood to reason he should be able to view them from an app or something.

"Are you fucking spying on Layla?"

"I'm not going to hide it from her," he growled, annoyed Gage had even asked that. Sure they weren't friends, but damn. He kept most of his annoyance in check because Layla adored the man who was engaged to her best friend. And okay, Gage had helped save her life, so for that alone Xavier would always feel indebted to the guy.

"Just checking," Gage said, laughing lightly under his breath.

At the humor in the other man's voice, some of the tension in Xavier's shoulders eased. "Sorry. It's been a long day."

"How long are you in town this time?"

"I don't know." Hell, he should leave tomorrow, put some distance between him and Layla as soon as possible. Because if he stayed, he'd be tempted to head right back to her place and finish what they had almost started. He was tempted to do that now. He could turn right around and...nope.

You'll get her hurt. Or worse.

He wouldn't do that to her. She deserved better.

"I'm sending the app and login stuff to your phone now. I created the app, and it's easy to monitor the cameras once you're logged in. I'll start monitoring them as well. Thanks for the heads-up."

"Thanks for this," he returned. "It probably is nothing but I'd rather keep an eye on her just the same." Especially since he never knew when he'd be called out of town.

"She's Nova's best friend. I'll make sure she's taken care of."

Though the words eased something inside Xavier, they also bothered him on a level he wasn't sure he could define. He didn't like the thought of anyone else, especially a man, saying he would take care of Layla. But he shoved all those feelings down because they had no place in his head right now. Or ever.

Layla wasn't for him. She deserved a man who could give her a real future. A man without blood on his hands.

* * *

From the shadows across the street, he'd watched Xavier walk back to his vehicle. It looked as if the hired killer had a weakness.

A woman, of all things.

It had taken a lot of digging, but he'd finally found Xavier. The place he was currently living in wasn't listed under his own name, but money could buy you a lot of things. Including information.

He'd also located Xavier's family. And he would go after them soon enough. But it was clear that Xavier was interested in this woman. Hurting her would create a different kind of pain for the hit man.

He'd watched them earlier tonight, and the way Xavier looked at her made it *very* clear he cared for her. Which meant she would be the perfect way to get to him. A bargaining chip.

In the end, she would die of course, but he wouldn't let Xavier know that.

No, he would let the man think he could save her, that he could get her back if he paid him enough money. Because he was going to take everything from Xavier.

Xavier's woman.

His money.

His family.

And then he'd kill him.

Xavier might only be a hired killer, but he'd still pulled the trigger that had killed his brother.

And now the bastard who had taken so much from him was finally going to pay. And he wouldn't be going after Xavier alone for this. No, Xavier wouldn't escape from him and neither would his woman.

CHAPTER THREE

—I get by with a little help from my friends.—

L ayla wasn't sure how she felt when she looked at the incoming text from Xavier. *Headed down to Orlando tonight for a last-minute trip, rain check on our shopping day?*

Her cheeks flushed with embarrassment even though he couldn't see her. Was he bailing on shopping because of what had happened last night? She knew his grandmother wanted to see him so maybe she was reading too much into it. Even so, she couldn't help feeling stupid over the whole thing in the cold light of day.

No problem, she texted back and left it at that. She was *not* going to ask him when he was getting back or mope over him. Because she was being ridiculous. Even if it was the wrong decision, as of right now she was going to be an ostrich and bury her head deep in the sand where he was concerned.

She texted Nova next, *Feel like a girls' night tonight?* They usually involved popcorn and hot cocoa, which were awesome. Plus she needed best friend time.

Nova replied almost immediately. *Yes! Let's invite some of the girls too. How about Hadley and Mary Grace? Not sure if Skye is free though.*

Perfect! She knew Darcy was out of town and Olivia had a big romantic thing planned tonight with her husband. She wasn't sure what Skye was doing, however. But if Skye could make it, she would. Although the Redemption Harbor Consulting gang occasionally worked odd jobs, and half the time Layla didn't know when they'd be in town.

Tossing her phone onto her countertop, she decided to be productive and take her mind off everything with Xavier. She'd been in contact with a great Realtor and there was no reason she couldn't look at places today. Especially since she wasn't going shopping with Xavier. It was time to get her life back on track. She loved being able to live here but she needed her own space that was just hers, and not provided by a friend's charity. Maybe it would make her feel more grounded to have something that was truly hers.

Something had to give. Hopefully a place of her own would help get her life back to normal again.

* * *

"Why are you guys looking at me like that?" Layla asked as she sat down at the table of the pizza joint owned by Mary Grace's husband.

Three sets of eyes all stared at her expectantly—Mary Grace's, Hadley's, and Nova's.

"Did something happen with you and Xavier? Nova said...maybe it did?" Hadley said, eyes bright with curiosity.

Layla was still getting to know Hadley and adored the college-aged woman who was a student in veterinary school. But Axel—Hadley's husband—and Xavier were actually friends, so she didn't want to open up too much. She knew the men had served together and then had done some other kind of work together later. Xavier had been vague on the details. Since she understood not wanting to spill every little detail about her own past, she'd never pressed him for more.

"Nothing happened. Literally nothing." She shot Nova an annoyed glance for saying anything at all. The traitor. Her best friend just smiled and picked up her hot cocoa.

"That man wants *something* to happen," Mary Grace murmured.

"Pretty sure he doesn't." Even though she desperately wished he did. And she was going to leave it at that because she was seriously too embarrassed to admit that she'd basically tried to kiss him—with the intention of jumping him—and he'd stepped back as if she'd tried to stab him. "And why are we talking about some guy anyway? It's girls' night."

"Because the opposite sex is entertaining," Nova said, shaking her head. As she set her mug down, the light glinted off her giant diamond engagement ring.

Layla was so happy her best friend had found Gage. She and Nova had met while in foster care and they'd been like sisters ever since. They'd formed a lifelong friendship, gone to college together, lived together during those years, and most recently her best friend had helped to save her life. There was no one in the world who deserved happiness more than smart-ass, wonderful Nova.

"Well if nothing is happening with you and Xavier, I kind of wanted to know if you would be open to a set up? As in for a date?" Hadley asked, surprising her and apparently everyone at the table, given the way they all looked at her.

Hadley grinned, revealing her elusive little dimple that just made her more adorable. When she smiled like that, Layla could clearly see the familial tie with her and her half-brother Brooks.

"What? I've been working at a new place and one of the rotating vets is really nice. He's good with animals, obviously," she said, laughing. "He's a little socially awkward sometimes, which I totally appreciate, and he's pretty new to the area. I get the feeling he's trying to make friends but it can be really hard. Something I understand," Hadley added. "And he's never been gross with any of the women at work. Which I know should just be common decency, but I've seen how some jackasses can be in the industry. He's just...a nice guy. And you're nice, so I thought you might like to meet him."

"Eh, setups are always kind of weird," Layla said. She wasn't interested in anyone but Xavier anyway.

"I know! Trust me, I know. But we've got that charity thing next Saturday and I know you don't have a date. I just thought we could invite him along and maybe he can get to know people, maybe network a little bit. You two could be each other's wing...people."

Layla chewed on her bottom lip for a long moment. When Hadley put it that way, it didn't sound horrible.

"He's really…kind of hot," Hadley added. "And I swear if you tell Axel I said that, I will deny it."

Layla snorted softly even as Nova gave kind of an evil laugh. "Now I have blackmail on you."

Hadley just rolled her eyes. "Whatever. It's not like he's as good-looking as Axel—no one is—but I'm just throwing it out there that he is a handsome, nice man. I'm not trying to set you up on some pity date or what-ever."

"Fine," Layla said, surprising herself. The truth was the thought of going to the charity function next week as a fifth wheel with all her friends was terribly depress-ing, so…why not? She was single and could do what she wanted. Not to mention after the insanity with her ex and what had happened with Xavier, it wouldn't hurt to put herself out there a little. Test the waters some.

"Fair warning, he tells 'dad jokes,'" Hadley added.

"Now you tell me, after I've agreed."

Hadley grinned, that dimple making her look even younger. "Oh, we can all ride together if you want."

"We'll see," Layla said. She liked being in control of herself when she went places. That way if she wanted to leave, she didn't need to depend on anyone else.

A lot of that was born from the way she'd grown up, so maybe for one night she could let go just a little.

Her phone rang, and when she saw the number on the display she was caught somewhere between excite-ment and panic. Xavier.

"Oh, give me a few minutes," she said, sliding out of the booth. Gah, she inwardly chastised herself for getting so excited about seeing his name. Seriously, butterflies were flapping around inside from just that.

Play it cool. Play it cool, she reminded herself as she headed for the entrance. *Pretend nothing happened, that everything's normal.*

"Hey," she said as she stepped outside the pizza place, hating that she sounded all breathless. The restaurant had outdoor seating, but given the weather, there was no one out here. The heaters were still going, however, so she sat under one.

"Hey, hope I didn't interrupt anything?"

"Nah. Just having a girls' night. So...I got your text," she started. Then she inwardly winced. Something about him turned her into a complete dumbass half the time. Obviously she'd received his text because she'd responded. She always seemed to say silly stuff around him though. It was beyond embarrassing.

"Yeah, I didn't want you to think I left because..."

So much for pretending all was normal. "Because I embarrassed myself?" she asked, massaging her temple.

"You didn't embarrass yourself. And..." He paused for a long moment, then, "I value your friendship," he finally said.

She winced. His words drove home the point that he definitely did not want a relationship with her. One other than friendship anyway. Because a man like Xavier wouldn't sit by idly and do nothing if he wanted a woman. If he was interested, he would let her know. He seemed like the kind of man who enjoyed pursuing a woman. Which just made her feel even crappier. First she was engaged to a monster, and now she was into her friend who didn't reciprocate her feelings. She'd definitely imagined that raw sexuality in his dark green eyes.

Stupid, stupid wine goggles!

"I value your friendship too," she said quietly. "And I hope I didn't do anything to mess that up?"

"No," he said quickly. "You could never do that. You're a beautiful woman, Layla—"

"Okay, let's not do this. Please. Look, I'm just throwing it out there that I'm totally embarrassed. I could blame it on the wine but I hadn't had that much. I wanted to kiss you and clearly that interest isn't reciprocated. I'm fine with that. I swear. But I really don't want to hear you talk about how beautiful or great I am. Let's just forget what happened." She was really laying herself bare here, but there was no need for anything else. She would rather rip the bandage off right now in one go, and get this conversation over with.

"Okay. But you are the most beautiful woman I've ever known," he said quietly.

She tightened her jaw for a long moment, fighting a sudden wave of stupid tears. She wasn't even sure why she was getting emotional. It wasn't as if they had ever had a relationship other than friendship. She was just being stupid right now because her life was in turmoil. Well, maybe not so dire as that, but it was certainly upended. "Thanks," she murmured. She wasn't sure what else to say. "So are you really in Orlando?" *Meaning, did you lie and blow me off?*

"Yeah. You were right about me needing to come see my family." She could hear the smile in his voice and knew he was telling the truth. She was surprised at the relief that slid through her, but it eased an invisible weight on her shoulders that he'd been honest.

"Good, then. Has your grandmother already fed you?"

He laughed, the deep sound like an aphrodisiac. "Like three times since I've arrived. She's trying to fatten me up."

Considering how built he was, she was sure he would just burn all the calories off by breathing. Not that she'd seen him without his clothes, but they had hugged enough that she'd felt everything he was hiding underneath his sweaters and shirts.

She shut that thought down really fast. "Look, I've got to go. I've been away from the girls too long, but thank you for calling. When you get back in town I hope we can start over and pretend everything's like it was before?" It depressed her, but having him as a friend was better than losing him entirely.

"Of course. I'll call you as soon as I'm back."

As they disconnected, she set her phone on the round, mosaic tabletop and stared at it as if it had the answers. Voices grew louder as the restaurant door opened and closed. Glancing over, she smiled as Mary Grace stepped outside, bundled up in her thick purple coat and rainbow-colored scarf wrapped around her neck.

"You look like you need a hug." Her breath was visible as she spoke, like little wisps of white smoke curling in the air.

"I'm pretty sure I do."

Making a sort of clucking, sympathetic sound, Mary Grace leaned down and wrapped her arms around Layla for a quick hug. "I take it that was Xavier?" she asked as she sat down.

"Yeah. I don't know why I'm being so emotional over this. It's not like I'm losing anything, because I never had it to begin with."

"So? The heart wants what it wants." She snorted. "I should know. Mine has wanted the same man since I was fifteen."

Layla half-smiled, because wasn't that the truth. She needed to get over Xavier. Or her feelings for him. She couldn't do this whole moping-around thing. She refused to. But that sexy man had gotten into her blood and she was completely hooked. "I know it's not technically a date next week, but I'm glad I said yes to Hadley's friend."

Mary Grace nodded once. "You'll have a good time no matter what. And you know Hadley wouldn't steer you wrong with this guy—neither Axel nor her overprotective father would let her set you up with someone they hadn't already thoroughly vetted."

That pulled a real smile out of her. Hadley's father was crazy overprotective. So was her husband. And brother, for that matter. They'd probably vetted everyone she worked with by now, including Layla's future date. "True enough."

No matter what, next weekend she'd fake it if she had to. She was going to dress up, go out with her friends and have a good time. *Fake it till you make it, baby.*

CHAPTER FOUR

—Nothing made sense until her.—

"It's rude to eavesdrop on people," Xavier said as he shoved his cell phone in his back pocket. One of his many cell phones. But this one was the most important because Layla had this number. And like a coward, he'd left Redemption Harbor earlier today because if he'd stayed, he wouldn't have been able to keep away from her. But it was for her protection that he'd left. And he'd been keeping an eye on her security cameras—and knew for a fact that Gage was too. That was the only way he'd been able to leave her, knowing that the Redemption Harbor crew were all looking out for her.

"It's not eavesdropping if it's your abuela," his grandmother said, hugging him from behind.

Laughing lightly, he turned away from staring out at the glistening pool in her backyard. She barely came up to his chest as he pulled her close. "So how much did you hear?"

"Enough." She pulled back and patted him lightly on his upper arm. "Come sit with me."

With coquito in hand—it didn't matter that Christmas was over, his family had at least three bottles left over—they sat at the patio table. He frowned when she pulled out a cigarette.

"You told me you stopped." He kept his tone mild, knowing she wouldn't respond well to anything else.

She shrugged and lit one up. Her dark curly hair was soft around her shoulders and peppered liberally with gray—which she claimed came from him. She probably wasn't wrong. She'd never bothered coloring it, saying she'd earned it. "I only have one every now and then. I'm an old woman. I get to do what I want." Her light accent grew a little thicker when she was annoyed. As usual, she had on a brightly colored long-sleeved top with loose, black linen pants, though tonight she had a thick wrap pulled around her that he'd bought her for Florida's pseudo winters.

He was tempted to take the cigarette from her but he knew better. She would definitely smack his hand away, and hell, she *was* an old woman. She could do whatever the hell she wanted. She'd earned it. "Fine. I'm going on record as saying I don't like this."

"Well, I don't like a lot of things you do, but you don't see me complaining." She arched an eyebrow at him, her dark green eyes sparking with defiance as she took a drag.

Touché. Quiet now, he leaned back in the chair and stared out at the pool again. Two giant floats—one fla-mingo and one rainbow—drifted across the blue water. She'd turned on the multicolored lights tonight so everything was bright. His abuela was such a tough woman. She'd basically raised him after his parents died, even when he'd been a horrible teenager. And she'd always loved him. Always. She'd let him know—loudly—when

she'd been disappointed in him, but he'd always been secure in her love. And he'd been a total shit who hadn't
deserved her. Hell, he wasn't sure why she still loved
him.

"So what is going on with you and this Layla?"

"Nothing." And that was the problem.

"You like her, sweet boy. Anytime you say her name,
your face changes. What's holding you back?" She took
another drag of her cigarette, blowing smoke in the
other direction.

The scent of it was as familiar to him as the back of
his hand. She'd smoked that particular brand on and off
from the time he'd been a punk teenager.

"She's too good for me." And that was what it boiled
down to. She was too good and he would just get her
hurt.

"She told you this?" His abuela straightened, all indig-
nant rage in a small package.

"No! She's sweet and wonderful. She would never say
something like that. She's... She's just too good for me. I
don't want to bring any trouble into her life. So I think
we should just stay friends."

She settled back against her chair. "But she likes you?"

He looked away. "She's confused."

Now she snorted loudly. "Confused? Oh sweet boy,
sometimes you are as stupid as your grandfather was,"
she said, affection in her voice.

His grandfather had died when Xavier was ten.
"Maybe it's just my gender in general," he muttered.

"This is very true."

His lips curved up at her matter-of-fact tone. "I'm glad I came home." For safety reasons he tried not to come to Orlando too often, and when he did he was careful about it. Very careful. No commercial flights, but private ones. Or he just drove himself from another location. But he needed to see his family. They kept him tethered to the world. Kept him from becoming someone he didn't like. Especially his young cousins. He probably bought them too many gifts but he didn't care. He'd gotten into his profession for his family, to take care of them, to give them the kind of life they deserved.

"You don't come home enough."

"Work keeps me busy."

She narrowed her gaze slightly at him, her eyes sparking. "So how are your *investments?*" she asked, the faintest hint of sarcasm in her words.

The rest of his family believed him when he told them what he did, but not her. She'd always seen through him. She might not know *exactly* what he did, but he figured she could guess. She'd found one of his weapons once and been enraged. She hadn't actually said anything, but she'd barely spoken to him during that visit, hadn't offered him food the entire time he'd been there, and had just had this general look of disappointment.

That knowing look in her wise, dark green eyes, so much like his own, had been what cut the deepest. As if she was disappointed in him. That was okay; he judged himself too. But through his work he'd made enough to pay to bring his family to Orlando and put them in a safe, gated neighborhood—far enough away from where they'd grown up in Miami and the gang he'd once been part of. And they would never go hungry, never want for anything. Everything was paid off and in his abuela's name. That knowledge helped him sleep at night.

He shook his head, banishing the thoughts. After that visit, he'd never brought weapons into the house again. Instead he left them in his vehicle, locked up in a secret compartment, or at the condo he owned but rarely used. Because when he was here, he stayed with his family.

"Business is fine." Fine, but tiring. He wasn't sure what was wrong with him lately but he was thinking maybe he was ready to quit altogether. Axel had done it. Why couldn't he? His family was taken care of at this point and he'd hidden enough away for their future. He just worried that it wouldn't be enough. His abuela had made sure he'd never gone hungry but he clearly remembered how worried she'd been for a few years when he'd been in his teens. He knew for a fact she'd gone without for him—he just hadn't appreciated it until he'd been older. After his parents died—taking away all the income their business had provided for the family—things had been rough. If they'd had life insurance it might have changed things. As it was, they hadn't and life hadn't been kind to his family for a while.

"You need to work less and date more."

"Date?"

"Whatever you kids call it today. And I don't care about dating. I want grandchildren. It sounds like this Layla wants you—"

"Abuela! Please don't go there." He couldn't think about Layla and children together. God, what he wouldn't give to make her his fully. The thought of her being pregnant with his child did something primal to him. Something he couldn't afford to dream of.

She lifted a shoulder and tapped her cigarette out. "From everything you've told me, she sounds like the perfect woman. She's even Puerto Rican. You're just being stubborn right now, just like your grandfather. Way too stubborn," she muttered.

Leaning over, he kissed her forehead. "It's a defect of mine."

She patted his arm gently, and for the first time he realized how frail she was. Her hand shook slightly as she pulled back, settling into her lounge seat. Maybe she was just getting older but he'd always thought of her as invincible.

"Is everything okay? With you? With the family?" His aunt, cousin and her two children all lived here, taking care of each other. The girls were in bed by now, his aunt was at bunco night with her friends and his cousin was binge-watching some show since her girls were asleep.

Smiling, she simply nodded. "Of course. We're wonderful. I miss you, but things are good. We all stay pretty busy. Natalia just took first place in her school's reading fair. And now Mia wants to become a lawyer when she grows up. Next week it'll be a dancer."

Sitting back, he listened to his abuela talk about his family, though he knew most of the updates anyway. But he loved hearing her talk in that raspy, no-nonsense voice.

This was why he'd come home. Okay, he'd come to escape the temptation of Layla, but being with his family always helped exorcise the demons inside him. At least for a little while.

CHAPTER FIVE

—Never underestimate the power of high heels and
lipstick.—

"Quit fidgeting," Nova said quietly.

Layla shot her best friend a sideways glance,
even as she tried to subtly adjust her bra cups. Or whatever the hell these things were. Her body was definitely
not made to wear these silly, sheer cups with no other
support. "I'm not."

"Okay." Nova shook her head as they stepped into the
giant ballroom filled with elegantly decorated tables, a
huge dance floor and a live band all under giant sparkling
chandeliers.

The theme was "New Orleans over the decades" so
there were brightly colored decorations everywhere and
everything seemed to sparkle. Little fleur-de-lis confetti
had been tossed on every table they passed, the only real
constant with the various centerpieces.

"Okay, maybe I am a little." She glanced down at herself, and while the vee front of her formal dress wasn't
exceptionally low, it was still way more revealing than
she was used to. Not to mention the back had an even
lower vee, hence the stupid cups holding her breasts up
instead of a full bra. At least the dress was snug so everything was staying put. For now. It just felt weird to not

have on a thick bra that supported all of her—and she needed it. She might be petite but she'd had breasts since she was thirteen.

"You look incredible," Nova said. "It's why I picked out the dress. Because I knew you would never pick it out for yourself."

Little champagne-colored beads and sequins were sewn everywhere so she sparkled when she walked. And against her darker skin, everything seemed to pop even brighter. So yeah, she could admit that Nova had nailed it. And it was true—Layla never would have picked this out for herself. It felt too bold and showy. From a young age she'd tried to blend into the background. Which hadn't always been easy, not when she'd developed so early. But she'd tried hard in an effort to be invisible to her mother—and her mother's boyfriends—and then later to the people she'd lived with in foster care.

"It's gorgeous. I guess I just feel weird being here on a setup." Like she was pathetic and couldn't get a date on her own. *Ugh.* Her date, Brian, was perfectly nice and had hung back outside the country club to take a phone call for work.

She'd ended up letting him pick her up because it made more sense for just one of them to drive, and if she hadn't, one of her friends would have insisted on picking her up instead. She didn't want to cramp Nova and Gage's style any more than she already had. At least she'd run into Nova on the way in.

Nova had already given her so much and was letting her stay at her house right now instead of renting out the place and making money. They had a lifelong friendship and she wasn't going to take advantage of that. Of course if Nova knew what she was thinking, she'd tell Layla she was being ridiculous. And okay, if she said these words out loud, she knew she probably was but she didn't care. Not to mention feeling like a third wheel could be emotionally draining.

Nova and Gage were so wonderfully happy together, as they should be, but it also brought up all sorts of ugly memories of Layla's mother telling her she was useless, a waste of space, "the worst thing to ever happen to me." Her mother had dragged her from Florida all the way to the West Coast, stopping in various states until they finally ended up in California. And she'd always made it clear Layla was unwanted—driving the point home in case Layla ever got any crazy ideas like maybe she was worthy of love.

What if...she never found anyone to share her life with? She wanted kids, something she knew without a doubt. She'd had such a shitty childhood and she knew she could do better than her own mother had. A freaking wolf could do better. Heck, it was part of the reason she'd gone into teaching. Kids deserved people in their lives who cared, and she wanted to be a mother so badly.

"Gage said that Brooks has a big table for all of us," Nova said, linking arms with her as they started moving through the mix of people.

Even wearing heels, Layla had to look up at her best friend because Nova was already tall *and* wearing heels tonight. She looked like a brunette Barbie doll. Tall, elegant, a true bombshell. Layla grinned as a few men did double takes when they walked by, staring at Nova as if they'd never seen a woman before. She didn't blame them. Her best friend was truly amazing. Not only that, she was also incredibly smart and resilient.

"So who's Gage talking to anyway?" she asked as they followed after her friend's fiancé and the man he was having a seemingly intense conversation with. He'd started talking to someone almost the second they'd stepped inside.

Nova lifted a shoulder. "I'm not totally sure, but I think he's a Realtor for industrial-type stuff."

Layla smiled as they reached the table to find most of their friends already there, though there were still a few empty seats. She wasn't sure how they were all going to fit, then Mary Grace pointed at the one directly next to them. "That's our table too."

The centerpiece was a large glass vase filled with multicolored beads. A collection of five intricate masks stuck out of the middle, the feathers and beads coming off them creating a waterfall of colors.

"You look amazing!" Hadley said as she approached, giving her a big hug. Her floor-length, dark green gown shimmered whenever she moved, the colors almost seeming to change to a lighter shade. "So where's Brian?" she asked, looking around. "Please tell me you didn't ditch him."

Layla let out a startled laugh. "Are you serious?"

"I'm joking," Hadley said. "Mostly. I know he can be kind of shy."

"He's taking a work call. He's not on call but I guess one of the other vets had a question. He was perfectly apologetic."

"Oh, of course. Everyone's always calling him for something. So what do you think of him?" her friend asked.

"He's very nice and polite." The kind of man she would bring home to meet her mother. If hers had been alive—and if her mother hadn't been such a raging addict made of pure evil who'd once tried to sell Layla to her dealer.

Axel strolled up next to them, a warm smile on his face. She'd come to learn that he didn't actually do big smiles, not like Hadley anyway. Everything about her was sweet and open, and he was kind of reserved, but Layla genuinely liked him. He gave her a sort of half hug and pulled back before sliding a protective arm around Hadley. "It's good to see you."

"You too."

From there she started making the rounds, greeting all of her new friends, then finally her date arrived at the table.

His sandy-brown hair was a little ruffled, probably from the wind outside, and his blue eyes were kind as he smiled at her. "I'm really sorry. They had an emergency and I couldn't ignore the call."

"It's fine," she said. "Trust me. I would probably judge you if you hadn't answered. You said the dog had been hit by a car?"

His expression darkened just a little as he nodded. "Yeah. But I think he's going to be okay."

"Well good, then." In her experience, animals tended to be nicer than most people anyway.

He glanced around at the two tables. "Do you have a drink or food yet? I can go grab you something."

"Sounds perfect. I've seen servers walking around with champagne trays."

"I'm on it. I promise to be a good date from this point forward," he said laughingly. And when he smiled, he looked boyishly handsome even though she knew he had to be in his thirties.

She smiled back, and wished she felt something for the man. Any sort of attraction. Just a spark, even. But nope, there were no butterflies in her stomach. No anticipation. No worrying what he thought of her. He seemed nice but she didn't care if he thought she looked incredible tonight. Why? Because she was hung up on one of her friends who didn't want her back.

Damn it. No. No, no, no. Xavier didn't get to take up any space in her head right now.

Even if she really, really wished he could see her. Because she could admit, even if this dress was out of her comfort zone, she did look kind of amazing. But no. There would be no more of that tonight.

She shook off all thoughts of Xavier. She wasn't going to let her own ridiculousness ruin tonight. Because she planned to have a good time. She didn't need a man to do that. Hell, she had a vibrator at home. And that was more than good enough for her right now.

* * *

"You're a great dancer," Layla said as she and Brian stepped off the dance floor. They hadn't left the floor for the last three dances and he was very clearly comfortable out there. Which was a rarity in her experience.

"My mom insisted I take classes," he said, seeming almost embarrassed. "She said I'd thank her later."

She laughed lightly. "Well you can tell her the lessons paid off." He was incredibly polished in the sort of way she recognized from kids who had grown up with money. She could be wrong, but ninety-nine percent of the time she wasn't. She'd grown up in the foster system and had attended one of the best public high schools in California, so she was pretty good at being able to spot money.

He had perfect white teeth, and a fading tan thanks to the chilly weather. Not that those things told her much. Well, the teeth did, because that cost money. But it was the way he spoke and the fact that he had a clearly custom-made tuxedo on—not some rental—and his shoes and cufflinks were Gucci. So far, he was knowledgeable on current events, and when he'd talked about vacationing with his family when he was younger, it had been to Europe. The guy was a vet so obviously he'd had a lot of years of school and was very bright. He was so open and warm and not in that skeezy, gross way she'd learned to recognize from a very young age.

It was easy to see why he and Hadley had become friends. Because Hadley was the same way. She almost reminded Layla of a little bunny rabbit from one of those Disney movies: sweet and innocent and you just wanted to be friends with her.

"So where are you from anyway?" she asked. He'd talked about his family in general terms but hadn't mentioned where he was from.

"Texas. Dallas."

She thought he'd had a hint of an accent but hadn't been able to place it. "Does your family still live there?" she asked as they threaded their way through the growing crowd to where their tables were located. All the glittering golds and purples made the entire place sparkle and seem bigger than it actually was.

"Yep. My parents still live in the same house they raised me in. And my sister lives two neighborhoods over. I get guilt trips often for moving here."

"Why did you?"

"The perfect job came up," he said as if he'd answered this question before. But there was a hint of something, maybe pain, in his tone, as he answered.

"So any other siblings?"

He nodded once. "Brother."

When he didn't expand, she didn't ask any more questions. She understood about not wanting to talk about yourself. It was why she usually put the focus on other people, deflecting from personal answers herself. Because her childhood had been shitty and no one wanted to hear about it. She wasn't embarrassed because it wasn't as if she could control the way she'd grown up, but she also didn't want anyone's pity.

"What about you? Any siblings?"

"Well Nova isn't actually my sister, which you can tell from looking at us, but she's family in all the ways that count." Wasn't that the truth. Nova really was the sister of her heart. "We pretty much grew up together."

"What about your parents? Where are you from?"

She cleared her throat once. Normally she was vague when answering questions by saying they'd died and she didn't often talk about them, but she didn't have the energy to lie or deflect. Not tonight, when he'd been so open and honest with her. "I grew up in the foster system, and honestly, it's not fun to talk about."

He blinked once but he gave her a smile. "Fair enough." He started to say something else when they reached one of the tables and she spotted Xavier next to Axel.

Xavier is here?

She blinked, wondering if she'd conjured him up in her mind. Nope. He was real and he was staring at her with an odd expression. What the heck was he even doing here? "Xavier!" she cried. "When did you get here?"

He seemed to shake himself out of whatever was going on in his head as he rounded the table. He pulled her into a surprisingly tight hug. It had been a week since the weirdness between them and they'd texted back and forth like normal so she really hoped all that was behind them. She couldn't bear to lose him as a friend. And hey, look at her on a date tonight. That should show him that she was all good.

"I just got into town this morning and Axel invited me. He had an extra ticket."

"That's great," she said, stepping back and putting some distance between them. Butterflies erupted inside her nonetheless because they were in the same vicinity. God, he smelled so good. She seriously wanted to bury her face in his neck... *Nope.*

Realizing she needed to introduce her date, she turned to Brian, who had a genuine, warm smile on his face as she introduced the two men. He held out a hand, but Xavier paused before taking it, which made her blink.

"Are you guys thirsty? I can grab all of us champagne?" Brian asked, looking between them.

"You don't have to do that," she said. He really was an attentive date.

He shrugged. "We've been out on the dance floor for a while."

Xavier made a sort of strangled sound before he cleared his throat. "I don't need a drink," he practically growled. His pale scar was pulled taut tonight, seemingly more vivid under the lights as he watched her date.

She frowned at him, wanting to ask what the hell was wrong with him. He'd made it *very* clear he wanted nothing from her other than friendship so this *couldn't* be about jealousy. If it was, that was insane. And she wasn't going to put up with someone jerking her emotions around. She didn't think he was like that, however, so something else had to be going on with him. Maybe he'd had a bad day or something. Or maybe something had happened with his family?

"I saw you two on the dance floor," Mercer said as he cut into their little group, a big, affable smile on his handsome face. The man was huge and she could see how he'd played professional football once upon a time. "Mary Grace keeps stepping on my toes, so I need a break. You feel like another dance, Layla?"

"I see my husband is lying." Mary Grace grinned as she hooked her arm through Brian's. "Why don't we show them how it's done?"

Grateful for the escape from Xavier's presence, she let Mercer take her onto the dance floor.

"So I know you're lying about Mary Grace's dancing. What's going on?" she asked as he spun her around once.

He loosely held her hand in his, his other giant hand on her waist as they swayed to the music. "Well, Xavier looked as if he was about to take your date's head off, so we decided to intervene. I called an audible."

She was certain that was a football analogy—even if she wasn't sure what it meant. Soccer was more her sport of choice. Layla was silent for a long moment, not sure what to say. Xavier *had* looked kind of annoyed. But he was so hard to read. "Men are frustrating," she finally muttered, not wanting to get into the whole Xavier thing now or ever.

Mercer laughed, the loud sound drawing a few looks from nearby dancers. "You'll get no argument from me there. I hear that enough."

"You really are surrounded by females." There was his wife, his baby daughter, and then everyone who worked at his restaurant, right down to the management, were women. And Layla knew that Mary Grace had a bunch of sisters who were always over at their place.

"Yep. And I wouldn't have it any other way."

"How's your new manager working out?" He'd recently hired a woman named Lucy to run one of his restaurants. Lucy was engaged to Leighton, one of the men who'd helped found Redemption Harbor Consulting, and her credentials were impressive.

"Perfectly. I read that businesses run by women see a higher profit, and I believe it. She's come up with some smart ways to bring in more customers."

Layla knew he hadn't been struggling to begin with. "That's great."

"It really is. Women are going to rule the world one day."

"I kinda hope so," she said, finding herself laughing despite her weird mood. It was hard not to be in a good mood whenever she was around Mercer or Mary Grace. They were two of the nicest people she'd ever met—they were what Nova called "relationship goals." But Layla was pretty certain that was never going to be her and...anyone.

Feeling as if someone was watching her, she glanced over at the side of the dance floor and saw Xavier staring at her with undisguised lust.

What. The. Hell.

Flustered and annoyed, she turned back to Mercer, determined to get her mind off Xavier. "How's that sweet baby of yours doing?"

And that was all it took for this giant of a man to practically melt before her eyes as he started talking about his daughter and how he was convinced she was a genius destined to run for president one day. She wasn't even a year and a half yet, Layla didn't think. But he was very proud of her. Seeing that kind of love on a grown man's face made her smile. And she could admit that good parents were her soft spot. It didn't take much to love a kid, and she'd never understood those people who brought children into the world then abused them or abandoned them.

Right before the song ended, Xavier slid in next to Mercer, so smoothly cutting in that she barely registered the transfer. She blinked in surprise as he pulled her close—too close—all those rock-hard muscles pressed up against her as he looked down at her. Too many emotions mixed together on his face for her to pinpoint just one, but the *heat*? Yep, that was definitely there. And it only served to confuse her even more.

"Who's your date?" he growled out with a surprising amount of annoyance he wasn't even bothering to hide. Like he thought this behavior was okay.

"Well, you know his name. He's a vet."

"How'd you two meet?" He looked around, as if he was scanning the room for some kind of threat before he focused that intense stare on her again.

She narrowed her gaze. "Why?"

"You just never mentioned him before."

"I didn't think it mattered." She looked away from him, feeling a little bad for leaving her date, but then she saw that Brian was talking to Nova and Gage so it eased some of her guilt. He was a grown man. She didn't need to pay attention to him the entire date anyway. "I'm sure you don't tell me everything about your travels." Like the women Xavier might be sleeping with. A weird kind of jealousy bubbled to the surface at that thought. She ruthlessly shoved it down.

He stiffened slightly in her arms. "What do you mean?" he asked, his movements slow and sensuous. For such a big man he moved with a fluid grace that surprised her. She wondered if that translated to bed, then internally cursed herself. She didn't care about that.

I don't.

"I'm sure you've been seeing other women, and I don't expect you to tell me all about your 'dates.'"

All the tension seemed to escape his body at her words, even as he made a derisive grunting sound. "I'm not dating or sleeping with anyone." He said the words as if her statement offended him.

And that was when she felt his very real erection brushing against her stomach.

Holy shit. Her gaze snapped to his. "Xavier," she whispered.

"I'm sorry." But he didn't sound or look the least bit sorry. In fact, he looked as if he wanted to eat her alive.

What.

The.

Hell.

CHAPTER SIX

—If Cinderella's shoe fit so perfectly, why did it fall off?—

"What is going on with you? You're acting like a jealous boyfriend...and now this? You're the one who made it clear you didn't want a relationship or anything other than friendship." Layla struggled to battle the hurt bubbling up inside her. She hadn't expected this kind of game-playing by Xavier. *Not him.*

"I know."

She waited for him to continue but when he didn't, she said, "So that's it? You *know*? I don't appreciate these mind games." And she'd expected more from him because of their friendship, so this hurt. Really, truly hurt.

He sighed, watching her intently. "I'm not trying to play any mind games."

"Are you sure about that? Because you're acting all weird because I'm on a *date*. What do you expect, me to remain celibate just because—"

He let out a soft little growl that made heat curl low in her belly. Oh God, that sound. She shouldn't like it at all. So now she was pissed at herself. "What?"

"Are you planning on sleeping with him?" There was a dark glint in his green eyes.

Oh, hell no. That definitely wasn't any of his business. "Did you just ask me that?"

"Well?"

She gritted her teeth, glad the music was so loud that no one else would be able to overhear them. "I'm not discussing this with you."

"Layla—"

"No. You made your feelings very clear. I'm fine with it. What I'm not fine with is you jerking my emotions around. That's not cool, *especially* since we're friends."

She'd been through enough and she wasn't going to add this kind of crap into her life. Xavier's behavior was worse though, because of their friendship—and because she felt a whole lot for him. More than she wanted to admit.

Before he could respond, she continued, "This is the last time we're dancing tonight. I came here with someone else and I'm leaving with him. If you don't like that, too bad. Maybe we need to reevaluate our friendship at this point." She stepped away from him as the song ended and could feel her cheeks flushing with anger. Her annoyance was definitely showing in her expression.

She'd never been one to hide her emotions well. Last year she'd had to hide how much she loathed her fiancé at the time because it had been a matter of literal life and death. If he'd suspected what she knew—that she'd seen him murder a DEA agent—she wouldn't be dancing in this exquisite dress right now. As it was, she wasn't in a life or death situation. And she didn't care about hiding how angry she was at Xavier. At least not to him.

She took a deep breath, getting her emotions under control as she made her way from the dance floor. It didn't take long to reach Brian, who was laughing at something either Gage or Nova had said.

He smiled when he saw her, all genuine warmth, clearly not bothered that she'd danced with a couple other guys. That was definitely a point in his favor. Not a jealous jackass. Not like someone else she knew. *Ugh.*

"I think I'm ready for that champagne now," she said, linking arms with him. For the rest of the night, she'd be tuning Xavier out as best she could. Which would be difficult, considering he simply had one of those presences. At least to her. For some reason her gaze was automatically drawn to him. Like those stupid moths and flames. She was a dumbass moth. *Ugh.*

"Good," Nova said, smiling. "You guys can grab me a drink too," she said, laughing as Gage swept her onto the dance floor.

"I hope you didn't feel neglected," Layla said to Brian as they headed toward a passing waiter. Out of the corner of her eye she saw Xavier near one of their tables, but she refused to look in his direction. She would not give him the satisfaction.

"Not at all. Your friends are nice. Hadley told me I'd have a good time and she wasn't wrong."

"Yeah, she's the best," Layla said.

"So the guy you were just dancing with..."

She tensed. "Yeah?"

"Is he an ex-boyfriend?"

"No. We're friends." And after tonight, maybe not even that. She couldn't take his hot-and-cold routine.

Brian gave her a look that said he didn't believe her. "Look, I'm not trying to come in between anything. Hadley said you were single—"

"Look, we're not anything. We really are just friends. I honestly don't know what's going on with him tonight. But I do need to be honest..."

"This is probably our first and last date?"

Oh wow, he read her right. "Yes?"

"Is that a question or a statement?" he asked laughingly as he plucked two drinks off a passing tray.

She grabbed one for Nova. "It's a statement. One that has nothing to do with you. I'm just coming off a really bad broken engagement. Clearly I'm not ready for anything else."

"I actually understand," he said, sadness filling those puppy dog eyes and his expression. Oh damn, why couldn't she be attracted to him? "But we're both friends with Hadley so I hope you and I can still become friends?"

"I'd like that. I'm pretty new to the area too," she said. "I'm still getting my bearings."

"Well if you're looking to settle in and maybe adopt a pet, I just started working with a new organization here. No pressure though," he said with a grin.

That actually sounded like a great idea. She'd already talked to Hadley about potentially adopting a dog once she figured out where she'd be working full-time. And this guy worked with an organization that fostered animals? It was a shame there was absolutely no attraction on her part—and she was ninety-nine percent sure there was no attraction on his part either. He didn't seem sad that she didn't want to go on another date.

"If I decide to adopt, I'll let you know. Hey, you want to see something funny?" she asked when she spotted Skye making a beeline for one of the food tables. Right now she'd use anything as a distraction from Xavier—who was thankfully talking to Axel and not staring at her.

"Always."

"See my friend Skye in the plum-colored dress?" she asked, referring to the sleek, auburn-haired woman in the floor-length dress that wrapped around her like a second skin. Her arms were toned in the sort of way that made it clear she worked out on a regular basis. Which she did. A lot.

Layla knew she mixed it up, but the one thing Skye always did was run *at least* ten miles a day. She nearly shuddered at the thought of all that exercise. "I guarantee every single time you look at her tonight she will either be picking up food from a tray, or already eating something."

"Seriously?"

"Oh yeah. It's hilarious. If she just had a crazy-high metabolism, I would probably hate her a little bit, but she works out like no one else I know." Layla had to respect that. Even if she had absolutely no desire to kill her body like that.

Almost on cue, Skye reached the table of hors d'oeuvres and picked up a small plate.

Layla grinned as she started loading it with little can-apés—and then Colt did the same. And Layla would bet good money that he'd loaded his plate up for Skye, not himself.

Just as she figured, Skye started popping them in her mouth one after the other. She did everything with precision. As if she knew she was being watched, she grinned when she saw Layla and smiled, heading their way.

Brian laughed lightly. "Well I can't eat all day every-day like that."

"No kidding. Me neither. But I also don't run half-marathons daily."

His eyes widened. "Holy crap."

"Right? She's who I want to be when I grow up."

And Skye really was amazing. In fact, all of the people Layla had become friends with since moving here were incredible. She felt so lucky to have met so many won-derful people. People who had literally put their necks out to save her.

If it wasn't for them, she would either be dead or in witness protection living some crappy life under an as-sumed name. She would have lost the one connection to her life who had been the only family she'd ever had. Nova. For that, Layla would be grateful to her new friends forever. They'd given her a new life. She wasn't going to waste it—and if she had to cut Xavier out of hers, it would hurt. But she would if she had to.

CHAPTER SEVEN

—If I could turn back the clock, I'd find her sooner.—

Xavier kept telling himself to turn right around and head back to the house he owned. It might be where he laid his head at night but it would never be home. Regardless, he had no business going to Layla's house right now. What the hell was he thinking?

That was the problem. He wasn't thinking. And what was he going to do if he went to her place and her date was there with her? *Fuck.* He needed to leave now. But the thought of another man touching Layla made him insane.

She was his. Had been from the moment they'd met. But he was no good for her. He needed to tell her that, so she understood.

Yeah, right. He couldn't lie to himself. So even as he parked, and jogged up the little stairs to her porch and found himself knocking on her front door—at midnight—he was still cursing himself. But he also wasn't walking away. Because apparently he had no control where she was concerned. He had no fucking sense either. He should have checked her outdoor cameras earlier, but by the time he'd even thought of that it was too late. For all he knew, her date was inside. He should have been more cautious as he'd driven up here, done a little drive-by of her neighborhood to scout out any threat. Instead, he'd zoomed over here like he had no damn training.

This had disaster written all over it.

The front door swung open and he found Layla in her pajamas, looking adorable. She had on pink plaid flannel pants and a skintight, long-sleeved pink T-shirt. He could just see the outline of her nipples. Her face was freshly washed and her long dark hair pulled up in a ponytail. Her amber eyes were filled with surprise as she stared at him. "What are you doing here?"

"Is that guy here?" he asked as he stepped inside as if he had every right to.

She made an exasperated sound and shut the door behind him. "You're letting all the cold in," she muttered as she locked the door. "And no. But if he was here, it would be none of your business. He could be in my bed right now for all it matters."

Oh, it mattered. "It is my business."

"You're going to give me an ulcer!" she snapped. He saw that hint of fire in her he'd only witnessed a few times before and it revved up something inside him. It made him wonder what she would be like in bed. Something he fantasized about all the time. Just the thought of her naked, under him, on top of him, it consumed him.

As he stalked toward her, she moved back toward the front door, still glaring at him. Without her heels on she was so much shorter than him, but her size didn't take away from her fierce expression.

"Did he kiss you?" he demanded, unable to let it go.

"So what if he did? Maybe I kissed him," she snapped. "Maybe I put on a little strip show for him to the tune of 'American Woman'! Maybe I let him touch—"

He cut off her words as he crushed his mouth to hers. Xavier didn't want to know if she'd done anything with her date. He didn't care. Okay, he fucking *cared*, but if she'd done anything with that guy, it didn't matter. The only thing that mattered was completely possessing her right now and wiping the memory of any other man from her mind forever.

She moaned into his mouth, her fingers digging into his shoulders as she jumped up, wrapping her legs around him. The way she clung to him surprised the hell out of him. She should probably call him out for being a jackass and showing up at her place at midnight.

His erection was hard between his legs, pressing against his abdomen, pulsing with need. She had to feel his reaction to her—and this was all for her. His entire body thrummed with energy, with the desire to thrust deep inside her over and over.

They needed to get to a flat surface. He desperately needed to taste all of her. To hear her moans of pleasure as she came against his mouth.

Xavier felt possessed with the need to have Layla even as he told himself this was insane. But as his tongue teased against hers, all common sense scattered like grains of sand at the beach. There was nothing else in the world but him and Layla. Nothing but right now.

And he needed to see her naked. Needed to taste her everywhere. Earlier tonight, in that dress, she'd looked incredible. Mouthwatering. And he'd wanted nothing more than to strip it from her body, to kiss and tease every inch of her. Now he was going to get the chance to imprint himself on her forever.

"Clothes off," he rasped out as he pulled back from her mouth, his breathing harsh.

She blinked at him, her expression as dazed as he felt. "What?" she whispered.

"I want to see you naked. Now." His voice sounded guttural, uneven. His words weren't even particularly dirty, but her cheeks heated up. Oh hell. He'd misread things. They needed to slow down now. "This is too fast—"

"No, I want this. I'm just...wrapping my head around this. Us."

That was all he needed to hear. He grasped the hem of her shirt and tugged it over her head. He hadn't come here for this. He'd come here to warn her away from that guy, but... Hell, maybe he had come here for exactly this. He couldn't lie to himself. He needed her like he needed his next breath.

Frozen in place, he stared for a long moment at her full breasts. Her skin was smooth, and her dark nipples tight little points, begging for his mouth. Groaning, he lowered his head to one, and as he sucked her nipple in his mouth she let out the sexiest, strangled sound as she arched against the door.

He couldn't remember ever being so hard in his entire life, but his cock strained impatiently against his pants, desperate to be inside her. Kissing her like this, teasing her, it was everything he'd been fantasizing about for months. And they'd only just started. He ignored the little voice in his head telling him this was a mistake. Because when he was touching her, everything felt right.

Her fingers dug into his scalp as he flicked his tongue against the tight little bud. She kept making little mewling sounds as she ground against him. He couldn't stop tasting her, couldn't stop any of this. He felt as if an avalanche was building up inside him, with nothing able to stop what they were doing. That stupid voice in his head telling him this was a mistake was just that, *stupid*. He wasn't listening to anything other than the driving need to make her come.

When he moved to her other breast, she made the sweetest little gasp of surprise and dug her fingers against him even harder. He liked the bite of pain. And he loved the feel of her against him and in his arms. Exactly where she belonged.

"I need more," she rasped out as he ran his hands down over her hips and ass, which was unfortunately still covered. But with any smooth skin he was able to tease, he savored the feel of her softness.

She was way too good for him, but she'd chosen him.

"Couch," he said as he lifted his head from her breast. They needed to get somewhere flat so he could splay her out. And upstairs was too far.

She gave him that dazed expression again, her eyes glittering with lust as he carried her to the living room. A bottle of water and her book were on the little table where she'd no doubt been relaxing.

As he stretched her out on the couch, he immediately hooked his fingers under her pants. She had on little yellow panties that barely covered anything at all. Thanks to the lace, he could see the little dark bit of hair covering her mound. Covering exactly where his mouth wanted to be. *Ah, hell.*

Slowly, he tugged the scrap of material down her bronze, smooth legs, tossing them to the side. God, she was stunning. Everything he'd ever fantasized about.

No, better. His fantasy didn't live up to the reality of her perfection. Why the hell was she with him?

He drank her in, wanting to memorize every inch of her, every dip and curve. When he caught her amber eyes, he was surprised to see nervousness in her expression.

Probably because he hadn't said a damn word. He needed to force himself to talk, to tell her exactly how perfect she was. "I know I've said it before," he said, his voice raspy and unsteady, "but you really are the most beautiful woman I've ever seen." There was more he wanted to say—so much more—but everything he thought of sounded stupid. And he wasn't a poet.

No, he was a killer who didn't deserve her, but here they were. And he was about to make her come. More than once hopefully.

His words seemed to matter because she gave him a soft smile as he lifted one of her ankles to his mouth. When he pressed his lips to her skin, she squirmed against the couch. Even from here he could see her glistening folds. She was already wet for him. Good, because he was rock-hard for her.

He was going to take as much time as he could, however, before he pushed inside her. He needed to give her this. She deserved everything.

By the time he made it to her inner thighs, she was trembling as she stretched her legs out, hooking one over his shoulder. "You're going to kill me," she said.

More likely he was going to die from pleasure. He couldn't respond as he slowly ran his tongue up the length of her slick folds. If he *did* die right now, he would be happy because he'd finally tasted Layla.

She arched her hips off the couch, bucking wildly as he teased her over and over again. He couldn't get enough of her taste, of everything. Her scent wrapped around him, intoxicating him, addicting him.

Though the addiction part was a foregone conclusion because she completely owned him. It didn't matter what happened after tonight—he would always be hers, and even if she ended up hating him once she learned what he was, it wouldn't matter. He was hers.

"I'm so close," she rasped out.

Her lust-filled words punched through him as he focused on her clit. The more pressure he gave, the wilder she rolled her hips. This was the single most erotic moment of his life, having her beneath him like this, being able to pleasure her like this.

Her back arched again as she started climaxing. It hit her so hard and fast that he wasn't expecting it. Reaching up, he pressed down on her stomach, holding her in place as he continued lashing her with his tongue. She struggled against his hold until finally she collapsed, spent. When he looked up at her, she had the most sated expression.

Her eyes were heavy-lidded as she smiled at him. "That was incredible," she whispered.

He couldn't find his voice as he crawled up her body. Instead he covered her mouth with his once again. He wanted to drown in her and right now he felt as if he could.

She wrapped her legs around him as they kissed, and when she reached between their bodies, rubbing her palm over his covered erection, he groaned into her mouth. He could come like this if he let them get too carried away.

Moving quickly, she unbuckled his pants, and when she grasped his cock he just about came on the spot.

"Sit up," she ordered softly against his mouth.

Though he liked being on top of her, he did as she ordered, easing off her and sitting up, his cock arching up against his stomach.

Surprising him, she knelt on the floor in front of him, taking his hard length in her hand.

For the life of him he couldn't find his voice. All he could do was stare at her as she started stroking him in a hard, sure grip. She met his gaze once before bending her head and taking him in her mouth.

A savage sound escaped him as she began sucking him, the wet heat of her mouth nearly enough to undo all his control. The pleasure was so acute, it flayed all his nerve endings.

He threaded his fingers through her hair, pulling the ponytail holder out so that her hair billowed around him as she continued her torturous, beautiful assault with the most perfect mouth ever.

He wanted to hold off but this was every fantasy he'd ever had. "I'm about to come," he managed to force out, wanting to give her time to pull back if she wanted.

To his surprise she continued, and it was too much for him.

He finally let go of his control, and she still didn't pull back, taking all he had to offer until he was completely spent, his head rolled back on the couch as she crawled into his lap.

"We could have been doing this for a while," she said tartly as she settled on him, her breasts rubbing against his unfortunately still covered chest. *Fuck.* He was still mostly dressed and she was naked.

All he could do was smile and gather her into his arms, searching out her mouth again as they lost themselves in each other. Soon enough he was going to take his clothes off too. But for now, he wanted to taste her again, to simply hold her like this.

Because he was pretty sure that when he told her what he did for a living, who he really was, she would hate him.

CHAPTER EIGHT

—My heart is not your dick, so stop playing with it.—

Groaning, Layla stretched her arms over her head as sunlight hit her in the face. She rolled over, expecting to see Xavier, but was disappointed to find his side of the bed empty. Reaching out, she patted it and found it cold so he'd gotten up a while ago.

She didn't hear her shower running so he must be downstairs. Hopefully he'd made coffee. And hopefully they could finally have sex. She'd wanted to before but he'd held back. But at least they'd had a talk about protection. They were both clean and she was on the pill so if they did get to that point, she wasn't going to worry about a condom.

She took her time getting up, feeling truly great. They'd fooled around again after what they'd done on her couch, and while she'd been ready for sex, he'd held off. Which okay, was probably a good thing. She didn't want to jump into anything too quickly though she knew she was ready for more with him. She had been for a while. Maybe that was stupid considering everything that had happened with her ex, but Xavier was nothing like that monster. Still, she wanted him to explain his hot-and-cold routine. Considering what they'd shared, she figured she deserved an answer.

After brushing her teeth, she headed downstairs, disappointed not to hear him or smell that familiar, rich scent of coffee. At the bottom of the stairs, she found the deadbolt unlocked, but the bottom latch locked and her security system had been set. He had her code so if he'd wanted to, he could have left and reset the alarm. And Lord knew she'd been so exhausted she would have slept through anything. She hadn't even heard or felt him leave the bed.

Not liking the sinking sensation in her stomach, she headed to the kitchen and found a short note from him. *I'm sorry. Something came up. X.*

That hollow feeling spread. He'd just...left? With no real explanation? Nothing about how great last night had been, or where they stood? She didn't need poetry or crap like that but...this note was cold, detached. She wouldn't even leave something like this for a non-friend. What the hell? He could have woken her up or texted her something more. Instead he'd left a stupid note. A sad, pathetic one at that.

God she felt stupid. Maybe she was overreacting but it angered her that he'd left after the night they'd shared. Like he couldn't be bothered to tell her to her face that he had to go. What if he left because he couldn't deal with what happened between them? It wasn't as if they'd had sex, so she didn't think this was a case of him getting what he wanted then bailing. And even if she was confused and hurt by him, she didn't think that was something he'd do. But clearly he had issues about something.

Crumpling up the paper, she tossed it in the garbage and headed back upstairs. She certainly wasn't going to text or call him. She wasn't going to play this game or deal with any more drama.

Nope. It was time to get her shit together and put him behind her. She had a meeting with her Realtor this morning anyway.

If this was how Xavier was going to be, she was done with him.

As the shower jets hit her, the warmth pulsing all around her, some of the tension left her shoulders. Not completely, and she could admit she was going to put on a brave face. It was a new day and that meant new possibilities. She was going to strive to be positive from this moment forward. She'd been dealt a crap hand many times during her life, but she had a heck of a lot to be thankful for. Like the fact that she was living rent-free in her best friend's gorgeous house and had the luxury to go look for a place while she got her career and life back on track.

Stay positive, she reminded herself. She'd fake it as long as she had to.

She hadn't done anything to drive Xavier away. If he'd left because of whatever…that was on him.

Still…familiar feelings of worthlessness bubbled up inside her. People she cared about rarely stayed, or they disappointed her—with very few exceptions.

Seemed Xavier was the same.

* * *

As Layla drove down the road, a new pop song played on the radio, but it barely distracted her. Today had been long. Good-ish, but still long. Well, the only good had been the time spent with Ellen, her Realtor. The stuff with Xavier? *Ugh.*

You're worthless. Layla could practically hear the words her mother had spat at her not long before she'd overdosed. She had been her mother's greatest disappointment. Considering her mother had been a coke addict, her opinion had been worth exactly shit. But for some reason the words her mother had thrown at her so often were tumbling around in her brain this evening.

And it didn't take a psychology degree for her to know why. Xavier hadn't reached out to her all day while she'd been out with her Realtor. And she hadn't been obsessively checking her phone. No, she had more self-control than that.

Barely.

But she'd been hoping she would hear from him—and that annoyed her. So she had definitely checked it when she'd gotten into her car after seeing the last cute bungalow cottage, and there had been nothing from him. So she pretty much knew what that meant.

Unless some crazy emergency had come up—and he would have reached out to her if so—he regretted last night. And he'd ghosted on her. Like a damn coward.

She wasn't sure if she regretted anything, but that familiar feeling of being rejected, of being told she was worthless, had settled inside her. And it pissed her off more than anything. She'd come a long way from that scared, unconfident little girl and she didn't like feeling vulnerable in this way. Hell, the reason she'd fallen for her ex was because he'd given her everything she thought she needed. Stability, a good life, and he'd worshipped her. It had all been lies in the end.

Shaking herself, she turned onto the two-lane highway that would cut her drive time in half. This road was usually traffic free, something she needed right now.

Wide open space.

A few miles down the road, Layla winced as some jerk drove up behind her, flashing his brights so that she could barely see. She flipped up her rearview mirror and slowed so the guy could pass her. Maybe it was a woman, but she was going to just bet it was some jerky dude. She was going a little over the speed limit so it wasn't like she was holding up traffic. And there was no one coming in the other direction so he could easily pass.

Her entire body jerked forward as the vehicle slammed into the back of hers. Heart in her throat, she clutched onto the steering wheel as he rammed her again.

Her tires skidded and slipped as she grappled for control of the wheel. But he hit her again, sending her flying into the snow-covered ditch.

A scream left her throat but was cut short as the airbag slammed against her chest, instantly starting to deflate. Pain punched through her as her car shuddered violently, the engine shutting off under the force of the impact.

Oh God.

Her chest hurt as she tried to get her bearings. With a shaking hand, she flipped her rearview mirror back down, but her car was at an odd angle and she couldn't see much other than snow and part of the road.

Some lunatic with road rage had just run her off the road, and who knew if he had a gun or some other weapon. She had to...call for help. She needed help.

Blinking, she reached for her fallen purse but froze when she saw the shadowed image of someone in her side mirror stalking toward her vehicle, something long in his hand. A tire iron?

Oh my God.

Her brain was fuzzy as she unstrapped herself, shoved at the deflating airbag as she scrambled over to the passenger seat. She fell against the glass of the other door because of the weird angle of her car, but she barely felt the impact as terror spread through her with jagged, icy talons. The only thing she had was pepper spray but she would use it against this guy.

With trembling fingers she grabbed her fallen purse. Her belongings scattered everywhere but her pepper spray was a little pink canister against the black floor mats. Clutching it tightly, she flipped the little switch so that the nozzle was free.

"Hey!" a muffled shout sounded nearby. Turning, she saw a flash of a couple different headlights appear.

The sound of squealing tires filled the air and the lights that had been blinding her disappeared. A giant truck sped away in the opposite direction and she saw at least two other vehicles parked a ways behind her. Some-one was running toward her.

Heart pounding, she crouched against the seat but some of her tension left when a woman appeared at the driver-side window, her expression concerned.

"Are you okay?" the woman shouted through the closed window. She had a thick beanie and a scarf on, but there was enough light that Layla could make out her delicate features.

"I think so," she called out, shaking a little.

The woman pulled on the door handle and Layla re-alized it was still locked. Crawling back up to the driver's seat, she felt around until she found the lock and pressed it open.

"The driver got away," the older woman said as she held it open. "I tried to get his license plate but it was covered in mud. Are you okay to get out or should you wait for the ambulance?"

"I'm okay." Layla grabbed her purse, wallet and cell phone, the only things she really needed. The other stuff on the floor could stay where it was for now. "Can you take this?" she asked, holding her purse out as she strug-gled to slide out.

"Of course. I'll hold the door open because I don't think it's going to stay open on its own," the woman said, taking her purse and offering an arm to steady her as she used her body to hold it open.

Layla's entire body started to tremble as she climbed onto the snowy embankment. What would've happened

if this Good Samaritan hadn't been here? Two Good Samaritans, she saw, when she noticed a man on the
phone, clearly talking to the police if his one-sided conversation was any indication. He gave her a half-wave
and continued speaking to the dispatcher on the other
end.

"Oh sweetie, you're trembling," the woman said, patting her upper arm gently. "Come on, let's get you back
to my car. You can warm up while we wait for the police.
Is there anyone you want to call?"

She started to say no but saw the smoke billowing out
from her completely smashed front end and nodded.
"Yes." She knew exactly who she was going to call.

CHAPTER NINE

—Friends become our chosen family.—

"So tell me again what happened," Skye said as Layla wrapped the blanket tighter around her shoulders. Sitting under the open back hatch of Skye and Colt's SUV, she watched as the tow truck pulled her crumpled little car out of the ditch.

Colt was talking to the officer, who he apparently knew because he'd gone to high school with the guy. Layla had already given her statement to the police and so had the two Good Samaritans who'd stopped to help her. And thank God they had stopped. Because she wasn't crazy. That guy'd had a tire iron and one of the witnesses had seen it as well.

It shook her. Why the hell had he targeted her? Had he planned to kill her? People and their freaking road rage. Some days she was certain the world had gone mad.

"I've already told you everything." And she was desperately close to bursting into tears, which was just embarrassing, but this on top of being rejected by Xavier was too much. She couldn't imagine Skye crying over something like this. No, Skye would have probably jumped from the vehicle and beat the shit out of the guy and made him regret ever being born.

"Sometimes repeating things helps you to remember stuff you might not otherwise." Skye's voice was soft and soothing. "Just little details that sometimes slip by. Remember, you called me for a reason."

"Not to get grilled," she muttered.

"Why did you call me anyway? Not that I'm not happy to help out," Skye tacked on.

"I don't know." She lifted a shoulder even though she knew exactly why she'd called Skye first.

"You don't know?"

"Fine. I called you because you are the scariest, most competent person I've ever met, and you're the only person besides Nova who I know for sure has my back. And I was feeling terrified." And she knew that Skye's presence would make her feel better. It was one of those psychological things, she guessed. She'd needed to feel secure in the world again. She wasn't saying that part out loud. This whole thing was horrifying enough without humiliating herself.

"Oh." Skye patted her on the shoulder once in an awkward sort of way that made Layla laugh despite the entire situation.

"It doesn't matter anyway. It was some random asshole with road rage. Maybe I wasn't going fast enough or maybe he didn't like the color of my car." Who ever knew with nuts? "I got really lucky those two strangers decided to do the right thing." She really didn't want to think about what would have happened if she'd been on her own. Maybe she'd have been able to escape with the help of her pepper spray, but she would never know.

"Maybe it was random, maybe it wasn't," Skye said matter-of-factly.

Her stomach tightened at the last bit, but before she could ask anything, Colt approached with the officer. The officer nodded at her politely. "Thank you for your statement, Ms. Ferrer. We're going to see what we can do, but without the license plate I'm not too hopeful anything will come of this. There aren't any cameras this far out that might have caught the guy. But we do have a good description of the truck and it's damaged from hitting you so we might get lucky."

She nodded. "I know. But thank you anyway."

"The tow truck is taking your car to a local place about five miles from here." He quickly rattled off the name. "Do you need a ride anywhere?"

"No, we've got her," Colt said. "She just needs a copy of the police report for her insurance company."

Oh, right. Layla hadn't even thought of that. She wasn't thinking of anything right now. In fact she felt kind of zoned out as she sat there and let Skye and Colt take care of everything. She was so used to taking care of everything herself but she was okay with letting them take charge. Probably another one of those psychological reasons she'd called Skye. The woman could be a force of nature and Layla was grateful to have her as a friend.

Once the police were gone, she let the blanket slide off her shoulders and started folding it neatly. Her hands were a bit steadier now, and since the EMTs had already looked her over she knew she was at least okay to get out of here. "I need to call my insurance company and get a rental. I have a substitute teaching job for most of the week, starting on Tuesday." It was Sunday now so she needed to get her shit together. "I need to get this squared away as soon as possible."

Skye and Colt shared a glance, their expressions impossible to read. It was clear the two of them were reading each other's minds. Or they might as well have been. They both looked back at her at the same time.

Skye spoke first. "Look, this probably was a random thing, but we don't like it. And I know you can get a rental through your car insurance company. But we've got plenty of company vehicles. They've all got bullet-resistant windows and tires. We'll feel better if you drive one of our company vehicles instead."

"Wait...what? All your stuff is bullet resistant?" Layla wasn't sure why she was surprised, considering what she knew of their exploits. And she was sure she probably only knew like five percent of what they actually did.

"Of course. It only makes good sense," Skye said. "And you won't have to wait to deal with your insurance company."

"Part of me thinks I should decline, but tonight scared me and I want to be smart about this. Do you think this has anything to do with my ex?" Layla couldn't imagine why, considering Brody was dead and no one he'd worked with had seemed to have any issues with her. She'd only been a threat to him when he'd been alive because she'd seen him commit murder. But she hadn't been a threat to any of his associates, most of whom were in jail now anyway for various crimes they'd committed.

She'd never had to testify against anyone or anything. She...didn't think she had enemies.

"It doesn't seem likely but we don't take chances with the people we care about. You're family," Skye said, patting her shoulder again in that awkward way.

For some reason those words combined with Skye's attempt to comfort her released the torrent of emotions she'd been trying to keep at bay until she was alone. Tears started streaming down her cheeks. "Stupid," she growled at herself, embarrassed as she swiped at her cheeks even as the tears wouldn't stop.

When Skye pulled her into a hug, she started crying even harder.

Her entire life could have changed tonight. Who knows what that guy had wanted from her? He could have killed her. Or worse. Oh God, it could have been so much worse. She'd been a single woman alone on this deserted highway with pepper spray to defend herself.

Her body shook with her tears as she let all of her emotions out on Skye's sweater and jacket. Eventually she managed to pull herself together, however. And she was only nominally embarrassed because screw it, if she couldn't be vulnerable in front of her friend, then what was the point of being friends?

Sniffling, she wiped away the last of the wetness and stepped back. "Sorry about your sweater," she muttered.

"You don't have to be sorry. That's what friends are for. Come on, let's get back to your place. We're packing you a bag and you're going to stay with Gage and Nova tonight at least."

"I don't think that's necessary." Sure, what had happened had scared her, but she had a security system at her house. A really good one. She didn't want to inconvenience anyone, especially after all Nova and Gage had done for her already.

"Well too bad. You're staying there. I already talked to Nova and she was pissed that you didn't call her. So good luck with that tonight."

Layla simply shook her head as she followed Skye around to the passenger side. She chose the back seat, even though Skye offered her the front. But she needed a little space to decompress.

The warmth of their SUV was comforting, taking away some of the chill that had seeped into her bones.

"So," Skye said after a long moment of driving in silence. "What's up with you and Xavier? Why didn't you call him? Or did you call him first and me second?"

"Skye," Colt murmured, giving his wife a pointed look.

Skye simply shrugged. "What? It will take her mind off things."

"I'm right here. I can hear everything you're saying," Layla said, amused even though she probably shouldn't be. It seemed Skye just said whatever was on her mind. "And I already told you I called you first—only you." She might have thought of Xavier, but no way was she calling him. Not after the way he'd ghosted on her. She was officially closing that part of her life. He'd proven to her that he couldn't be trusted to be there for her when it mattered.

"You're totally deflecting but I'll let it go for now."

"Thank you. Later I'll tell you what a dickhead he is," she added.

"Oooh, you're not making this easy to let it go, but okay."

Smiling to herself, Layla laid her head back against the seat and closed her eyes. It wouldn't take long to get to her place and pack. Then she needed to decompress at Nova's. To simply be quiet with her own thoughts. As she closed her eyes, however, all she could see was that guy, that terrifying shadow, stalking toward her with a tire iron in his hand.

She knew more than most that there were really bad people in this world, but for some reason she was still shocked by what had happened this evening.

* * *

He cursed to himself again as he pulled into the parking lot where he planned to get rid of his stolen truck. Walmart was as good a place as any to ditch this thing, and he needed to put distance between it and himself. Didn't matter that he'd been careful about stealing it originally or that he'd covered the license plate with mud. He wasn't getting caught. Not when he'd come so far.

And he'd been so close to taking her.

Xavier had left her place early this morning but *he* hadn't been able to make a move on her before then since she'd been with that real estate agent all day. Sure he could have killed the other bitch and then taken the Ferrer woman, but he wanted this as clean as possible. He hadn't wanted anyone to know she'd been kidnapped for a while.

Then when Xavier realized she was missing, his panic would set in. Then dread. Oh yes, he was going to suffer. And so was she.

And that stretch of road had been fucking perfect. There would have been no witnesses, no worry about any CCTVs, no nosy neighbors. But then two vehicles had turned off a side road at the last moment and ruined everything.

He'd contemplated simply killing them too but that made things far too messy. So far there was no way Layla could know this had anything to do with Xavier. For all she knew it was some random attack. Some asshole with road rage. That was the more likely assumption for anyone to make.

Later he'd try to get a hold of the police report. Hell, not try. He *would* get it. He had enough money to throw around to get exactly what he wanted. He could have hired someone to come after Xavier but he was doing this himself. Because everything about this was personal. Xavier had killed his family, and while it had been just a job for that asshole hit man, it was personal for *him*. And he was going to show Xavier that everything was personal. That fool thought he could get away with taking from him. He was going to find out what pain really meant.

However, he needed someone to do grunt work—and he couldn't be in two places at once. He would just have to see how things played out. But one thing he knew: Layla Ferrer was very clearly someone who mattered to Xavier. Otherwise he wouldn't have stayed the night. Xavier didn't ever fuck on jobs. Or at all, according to his research. So this woman, yes, she meant something to him.

He'd done enough research into the man to know that he didn't have any vices. Not prostitutes, escorts, drugs. Nothing that could be used against him.

Nothing but Layla Ferrer. She was Xavier's Achilles' heel.

And she would be his downfall.

CHAPTER TEN

—When you love someone you protect them.—

Skye crossed her arms over her chest as she looked at the multiple screens above Gage's workstation. "What've you got?"

"I hate to say it, but it's not much. I looked deeper into anyone connected to Layla's past who could potentially hold a grudge. But nothing is pinging. There are a lot of maybes, but...nothing that makes sense."

"It could just be a random act of violence." Skye knew there were enough of those everywhere. The world was filled with monstrous assholes who cared little for human life. Something random could offend them that would make practically zero sense to most people, but to them, they'd been wronged or slighted.

Next to Skye, her husband frowned as he looked at the screens, though she didn't think he was actually seeing anything. "I still don't like it. The witnesses said there was mud on the license plate, which feels very calculated. *Premeditated.* And I just got a call from my high school buddy that the cops found the truck abandoned in a Walmart parking lot."

"And?" Gage turned around in his chair.

"And they tried to take fingerprints from normal areas—steering wheel, door handles, the usual—but they came up with nothing. After that they dusted everywhere and there are no prints in that truck."

"No prints *at all?*" Skye asked. Only pros could wipe something that clean.

"Nope. The guy who owns it reported it stolen a few days ago. And he has an alibi for the time of her attack. A solid one. And I doubt the guy would have randomly attacked Layla regardless—I'll let you read his info later. He doesn't fit the profile."

Skye didn't like the sound of this at all. Random sucked, but it was better than the alternative. "Maybe it's connected to one of us? Maybe Xavier?" She wasn't sure if that was a stretch or not. It wasn't as if Layla and Xavier were dating, but they were...well, they were something.

"Yeah, I could see that," Gage said. "I could see Xavier having an enemy who wanted to use her to get to him. I mean, from what research I've done he's very careful, but the guy has got to have enemies."

"What has he said about the whole situation anyway?" she asked Gage since Layla was currently staying with him and Nova.

"Nothing, because I'm pretty sure she hasn't told him about her attack."

Skye frowned at that. "Why not?" Dammit, she knew she should've pushed Layla last night about what was going on with her and Xavier.

Gage lifted his hands in mock surrender. "No idea. And...I just told Nova what he does for a living. I'd assumed she knew but after a conversation last night between the three of us, I realized Nova didn't know he's a hit man either. I waited until it was just the two of us and told her."

Skye frowned. "How did she not know?"

"It's not like I talk about the dude often. He's come up maybe once when Nova made a smart-ass comment about him regarding Layla. I sometimes forget she's not here for all of our meetings."

"How pissed was she when you told her?" Skye didn't bother to hide her smile.

"We're not gonna talk about that," Gage murmured. "But she's going to tell Layla if she hasn't already."

Skye turned around and looked at Axel. "Have you talked to him since the party?"

He shrugged. "We talked—about weapons mainly. Nothing concerning Layla."

She was silent for a long moment. "Let's table what happened with Layla for a minute. Have we decided if we want to recruit Xavier or not?" Skye's instinct told her it was a good idea. She'd already known who he was through reputation long before they started Redemption Harbor Consulting, and before she'd met most of the crew. But she'd never actually met the guy until recently. And she knew he did contract work for the CIA right now. She also knew he took jobs on his own and that he was financially secure. His profession aside, she liked the guy.

"I don't know if we're to that point yet," Brooks said carefully, the first words he'd spoken this morning. The former sniper was almost always laid back and quiet.

"You don't have to mince words just because I'm in the room," Axel said. "Because I agree. I like Xavier. A lot. I served with him and I would trust him with my life. Hell, I would trust him with Hadley's life. But I don't know that he would be a right fit for us. And if we do recruit him, there's no going back. So we need to make sure he's right long term."

"I agree," Skye said. "And I want to go on record as saying that I foresee him being a fit with us. If he ends up with Layla anyway. Because if he does finally pull his head out of his ass and make things official with her, he'll stop doing hits." Skye wasn't sure if the man was capable of that first part, however. Some people weren't wired to have long-term relationships.

"You're very sure of that," Savage murmured, glancing at Brooks—his best friend.

"I am sure," she said. "If he settles down with her, he's not going to keep doing what he does." That was just simple logistics as far as Skye was concerned.

After that they talked about a few jobs they were considering taking around the country—most of their work was stateside. From there things circled back to Layla again.

Skye didn't like anything that had happened, but since she couldn't put her friend in bubble wrap and stow Layla away in a safe house, she had to be smart and rational about their next steps.

Because if she pushed Layla too hard, the woman would push back and just get all stubborn, potentially putting herself at more risk.

Maybe the crew wouldn't be the ones who needed to push her on this subject, however. As an idea formed, she brought it up with the group.

* * *

Out of breath, Xavier turned off the treadmill as he heard his cell phone ringing. He recognized the ring tone as Axel's. Normally he preferred to run outside, but it was icy today and he'd done about ten miles so far. He didn't normally run this much, but something had to ease the tension inside him. Unfortunately, running wasn't it either. All his muscles were bunched tight, he couldn't relax—he couldn't do anything other than obsess over Layla and how much he'd fucked up. How much he was *still* fucking up by not reaching out to her.

Because he was a coward. And he knew it. He'd run from her. For her own safety, but he'd run nonetheless. *Fucking coward.*

"Yeah?" he said as he turned his Bluetooth on.

"Hey, jackass," Axel said by way of greeting.

He paused, towel in hand. "What the hell did I do to you?"

"Nothing. I'm just wondering why you haven't been over to see Layla after what happened." Axel's tone was razor sharp. Disapproving.

Ice slithered up his spine. *Happened?* "What do you mean?"

There was a short pause, then, "She hasn't told you?"

"Obviously not," he snapped out, impatient. "Is she okay?" He ran the towel over his head, already leaving his home gym and headed to his bedroom. If something was wrong, he needed to get to her. Even if he had screwed things up.

"Some asshole ran her off the road and we're not so sure it was random."

"Details," he snapped, tension buzzing inside him like angry bees. Axel needed to get to the point right fucking now. And it sounded like Xavier might need to kill someone.

"She was headed home after looking at houses with a Realtor on Sunday when some guy ran her off the road. She landed in a ditch, airbags deployed, and when she looked in the rearview mirror, she saw that the guy had some kind of weapon as he came toward her, but by-standers scared him off. She told the police it looked like a tire iron."

Oh God. His heart stopped beating. That had happened Sunday? It was Tuesday now. "She's okay though?"

"Yes," Axel said. "Let me finish. There were two civilians who stopped and helped her. They corroborate the tire iron sighting. Then Skye and Colt came and got her. Right now we've got her in a company vehicle—it's bullet resistant and has trackers on it—and she's staying with

Nova because she's upset, understandably. I just wondered why you haven't reached out to her. Thought it was kind of weird, considering you guys are friends. Also, Hadley and Skye are making me call you."

He snorted softly. Hadley was Axel's wife, and Skye was one of the man's best friends—she'd been the best woman in his wedding. Both intimidating women—in very different ways. "Layla didn't let me know."

"Any reason she didn't?" Oh yeah, that was definite censure in Axel's tone.

"Other than I'm a jackass?" Because this was on him. He knew exactly why she hadn't reached out to him.

Axel just grunted in response.

Xavier paused for a long moment as he leaned against his bathroom counter. The only reason he hadn't already run out of the house was because he knew Layla was okay. Now he needed to get his head on straight in more ways than one. "How did Hadley deal with things when you told her what you used to do for a living?" Xavier had never asked Axel all the details but the sweet vet student was Axel's polar opposite. He couldn't imagine she'd taken it very well.

"Surprisingly, she took it fine," Axel said. "She's made of tough stuff, my Hadley."

"I don't know how to tell Layla what I do," he blurted. "I like her. But...I don't know how to admit my profession to her." Or his past. He hadn't even told her that he'd been in a gang. God, he was a fucking liar who wanted a woman who was too good for him. But he couldn't seem to cut ties and leave, even for her sake, to just ditch Redemption Harbor for good. Literally nothing was keeping him here except her.

But he couldn't walk away. Even if it was better for everyone.

"You planning on retiring anytime soon?" Axel asked.

"I don't want to do this the rest of my life." That much he was sure of. He was tired of killing, tired of looking over his shoulder...just fucking tired.

"Then make a decision. I have no idea how she'll take it when you tell her what you do. But I honestly can't imagine her staying with you if you continue to do it. I don't know her well enough, however."

Yeah, well, Xavier knew her and she wouldn't put up with that shit. He wasn't certain she could ever look at him the same if he told her what he did for a living. The thought of that made those bees come back, only this time they weren't angry, just agitated. He rolled his shoulders once. "You're certain she's safe now?"

"*Yes.* But we're trying to figure out if this was random or something more. Is there any possibility this could be connected to you?"

The ice from earlier slid its tendrils out even further, wrapping around his chest and squeezing so that it was hard to breathe for a moment. That was his worst nightmare. Layla being hurt because of him. Or hurt at all. But because of him? It was why he'd left her place. Part of the reason anyway. If he'd stayed, if he'd fallen even further down that rabbit hole with her, he'd have never walked away. And she would be in danger if it became known

she was his. "I'm careful. But I have enemies." Most of
them were dead, thankfully.

"We're trying to nail down who might have wanted
to hurt her and so far no one from her ex-fiancé's past is
popping on the radar. And she doesn't have any actual
enemies. She's a teacher."

"I can get together with Gage. Would he be willing to
go over some of my files—"

"Of course. That's another reason I'm calling. If we're
going to figure out where this threat is coming from, if
there even is one, we need to know who *your* enemies
are. And anyone you've targeted in the last year. Maybe
two years. Which means you're going to have to give
over personal information, something I know won't be
easy."

"I'll do it for her." He didn't like feeling vulnerable or
giving out any details about his job or past but if someone had targeted Layla because of him, he'd lay his entire
life bare.

"Another thing, she's got a substitute teaching job this
week. She starts today. Whatever time the school opens,
seven I think."

"What the hell?" It was almost seven. Why the fuck
had Skye and the others let her take the job?

"There's nothing that says this was a targeted threat,
and it's her life. I'm just telling you what I know. Also,
we've got eyes on the school. She's okay."

Okay, then. He could breathe for now. If Axel said she
was being watched, then she was all right. And nothing
had pinged on the motion detectors outside her house or

he would have received an alert to his phone. So would have Gage, for that matter. "All right. Do you think Gage is up?"

"He's definitely up. We've already had a meeting. It's his call but he'll probably ask you to come to our office and we can start going over things. We all want to make sure this was just random. And if it's not, we all want Layla safe."

"Okay, thanks. I'm going to call him." Once they disconnected, he took the fastest shower known to man.

Even if he hated revealing things about his past, especially illegal things he'd done, he'd do anything for Layla.

Anything to keep her safe. Including risking losing her forever by coming clean about his past.

CHAPTER ELEVEN

—I hate it when I have to be nice to someone I want
to punch in the face.—

"So how was your first day?" one of the teachers
asked Layla as they stepped out into the teachers-
only parking lot. She thought the woman's name was
Kristie.

"It was a great class," she said, meaning it. She really
liked the school. And elementary-aged kids were her fa-
vorite. They were so sweet and eager to learn at this age.

"There's an opening coming up in the next month,"
the woman said, smiling. "It's not common knowledge
yet, but I'm just giving you a heads-up in case you're
looking for something full time."

"Thanks." The breeze picked up and she tightened her
scarf. "I'm Layla, by the way."

"Kristie. I teach third grade."

"Nice to meet you. Kindergarten for me."

"Are you working all week?" the woman asked.

She nodded. "Today through Friday. Unless they
need me longer."

"Well it's a great school to work at. The principal is
new this year and we all love her."

"That's good to know." She'd already done some research of her own and had discovered the same thing.

The principal of a school could really make or break the decision of where she wanted to work.

It was basically the same with any other job. A bad manager could ruin an otherwise fantastic job. But the current principal was young, smart, and had an impressive résumé. All those things could mean nothing if she was crappy with her teachers and students, but Layla had heard otherwise.

As she weaved her way through the row of cars, she frowned when she saw that her vehicle wasn't where she'd left it. What the heck? Could someone have really stolen her borrowed car? *Gah.* She seriously wasn't going to tell Nova or Skye that the dang SUV had gone missing. Maybe...she'd parked it somewhere else? This was like icing on top of the crappiest cake ever. *Bah.*

She glanced around the parking lot then froze when she saw Xavier leaning against his SUV. He was half hidden by a truck, one of those big F-150 monstrosities.

Anger immediately popped inside her at the sight of him but something could be wrong. There wouldn't be any other reason for him to be here. Actually, how had he known she was here at all?

Frowning, she hurried over toward him. "What happened? Is it Nova?" *Hell.* She pulled her cell phone out of her purse and turned the volume up, but didn't have any missed calls.

"Nova's fine, but you're coming with me." His expression was dark, his scar pulled taut as he carefully watched her.

She blinked. "Excuse me? Why are you here? And where's my...the company's vehicle?" She'd driven an SUV that Skye had dropped off to Nova's in the wee hours of the morning and it drove smoothly. Not to mention the insulation must be great because she could barely hear anything outside it. It had been like driving around in a warm cocoon.

"One of the crew picked it up, and I'm taking you to a safe house."

"Are you out of your mind?" Like she was just going to go with him with no explanation after he'd ghosted on her?

"I heard about what happened."

She glanced behind her and saw two teachers talking on their way across the parking lot. So far they hadn't seemed to notice her or Xavier but she was definitely not having this conversation out in the open. If she ended up wanting to work here, she didn't ever want to be the subject of gossip.

"Come on," she muttered, veering to the passenger side of his SUV. There was no sense in arguing over the fact that the other SUV was gone. Because it was gone and she had to adapt. That didn't mean she was going anywhere else with him once he took her home—or to get another vehicle. And she had a whole lot of questions she wanted answered too. "Tell me what the heck you're doing here," she snapped as soon as he got into the driver's seat and started the engine.

"With what happened, I'm taking you somewhere safe. You don't need to be out in the open."

"Did they find something new? Does Gage not think it's random?" Her heart rate kicked up as she thought about being targeted because of her ex. Her stupid, dead ex-fiancé who might now be hassling her from beyond the grave.

"We don't think it's anyone from your past. But I have a long list of enemies. It's a possibility that you were targeted because of me."

She gaped at him. "Why on earth would you have enemies? And is your family okay?"

He shot her a quick glance as he drove, surprise flickering across his otherwise hard features. "I've already moved them to a safe house."

Uh, what? "Safe house? Okay, so you're not in finance or investments or whatever, are you?" Skye had been right, he really was dangerous.

He was silent, but his jaw ticked once.

"You're not going to answer me?"

"Not now. Just...let me get you to the safe house and I'll tell you everything."

"Well I'm not going anywhere with you, so you can take me back to Gage and Nova's place."

"You would put your friends in danger?"

She froze at his words. "You're serious? You think being there would put them in danger?" Seriously, what the hell was going on?

"At this point I don't know anything. But I don't think it's worth taking the risk."

What the hell had Xavier done?

She was quiet as she digested his words, thinking of what she needed to do. If what he said was true—and that was a big if because he wasn't telling her much—then she needed to talk to Nova and she needed to cancel work at the school for the rest of the week. She could make up a family emergency but she hated doing that. Hated lying in general. Jesus, would her life ever get back to normal? "You know that you showing up like this without any warning is completely insane, right?"

"I am aware."

She let out a growl of frustration. "I have more questions, but do you also know that you are a giant jackass for sharing that amazing night with me and then ghosting me like that?" She was shaking as she practically shouted the question at him. She wanted to know more about why he'd randomly shown up like this but seeing him now had all her rage sparking into a giant fireball. And she wanted to throw it all right at his face.

"I'm also aware of that. You're way too good for me," he muttered.

She snorted loudly. "Are you saying that's why you left? You're so full of shit. I don't want to hear any crap like that. You left because you're a jerk and not who I thought you were. *Clearly.*"

He sliced her a sharp look. "You're right. I'm not who you think I am. I'm not a good man. I've done a lot of bad things."

She narrowed her gaze at him, so many things she wanted to say on the tip of her tongue. But she took a deep breath. Deep down, she'd sensed an edge about him, and Skye had told her he was dangerous. She'd just ignored that because he had kind, soft eyes and she felt safe around him. Yep, she was definitely a dumbass moth. How many times did she have to get burned to get her head on straight? "How long do we have to be in this safe house or whatever? And more importantly, *why?*"

"I don't know."

"All right, then," she muttered, pulling her cell phone out of her purse. It was clear he wasn't going to answer everything. Completely ignoring him, she called Nova.

Her best friend answered on the first ring. "Xavier pick you up already?"

"You knew he was picking me up?"

"He kind of insisted."

Her stomach tightened. "How serious is this thing? I thought it was just a road rage incident. What's going on?"

She was silent as Nova filled her in on everything, including the fact that the stolen truck had absolutely no fingerprints. That was super weird but she wasn't sure how much stock she should put into it. It seemed to bother Nova a lot, however, so she was going to take it seriously.

When her friend was done, she said, "I can't go through what I did again. I can't live in fear and in hiding for an indefinite amount of time." Obviously if she had to, she would because she liked breathing. But...ugh.

"I know," Nova said, letting out a harsh sigh. "This is Gage's number one priority. *Our* number one priority. The whole team is working to see if we can figure out what's going on. And Xavier has given us a lot of information on people who might want to hurt him through you."

She made a sort of humming sound at that. Since she was sitting directly next to him, she was going to keep her smart-ass comment to herself.

"What exactly has Xavier told you about what he does for a living?" Nova asked.

"That he's in investments." She snorted, at this point knowing that was a lie.

Nova was silent for a long moment. "Look, you are my best friend. I didn't know what he does for a living until very recently. It's not investments. Do you want me to tell you?"

She glanced at Xavier and frowned. Every fiber of her wanted to know exactly what he did for a living. But she wanted him to tell her himself—and he'd said he would once they got to a safe house. "No. He's going to tell me himself. Right?" she asked Xavier.

He grunted an affirmation.

"Are you sure?" Nova pressed.

"Will I be safe with him?" Because that was pretty much all that mattered at this point.

Xavier sliced her a hard look, and there was almost something like…hurt in his gaze.

"He'll keep you safe. That I'm sure of. He…cares for you. It's the only reason I was okay with him picking you up. He'll take a bullet for you, girl. He might have screwed up, but he will make sure you're protected and you'll be his number one priority. While he's keeping you safe, we're going to make sure you stay that way."

"Thanks," she murmured, even if she wasn't sure about the whole "take a bullet for you" comment. She sure as hell didn't want that. There would be no bullets flying regardless.

They spoke another few moments, and when she disconnected Xavier said, "You're going to have to ditch your phone. I've got a bunch of burners for you—"

"Are you really going to tell me what you do for a living, or is my best friend going to have to tell me? Because I'll call her right back."

"I'll tell you." His words were clipped and his expression remote as they pulled down a residential street lined with big oak and magnolia trees—most of which hadn't lost their leaves. Smoke curled in the air from a few chimney tops but no one was out walking, making the street feel remote.

"Where are we?" she asked when he didn't continue. The man was determined to make her play twenty questions.

"I own this property."

Okay. "Tell me who you really are and why you've treated me so badly."

He let out a long sigh as he steered up the driveway to a large ranch-style home. "I never meant to treat you the way I did. I never should have touched you at all."

"First of all, I'm angry that you ghosted on me, not because of what we did." What they'd done had been incredible, but she wasn't going to think about that now.

It pissed her off that he'd brought her so much pleasure, that he'd learned her body so quickly—that she wanted more. But it pissed her off more to be used and thrown away. To be treated as if she was worthless.

He scrubbed a hand over his face as he shut the garage door behind them. "I know. What I did was beyond messed up. And I'm sorry."

To her horror tears sprung to her eyes so she turned and looked out the window at the interior of his basically empty garage. There were a few paint cans in one corner and a couple shelves with tools but that was it. "We were friends. I expected so much more from you."

"I know," he rasped out. "And I truly am sorry. I understand that we can never be friends again. And in light of all this I think that's probably a good thing."

"Why?" she asked, turning to look at him as she composed herself. She didn't want to lose him entirely. She'd missed him.

"Someone was digging into your personal files—and mine. Gage found traces of information linking both searches to the same person. They were digging deep into your life and as much of mine as they could."

No. Not again. She laid her head back against the leather seat. "I just want to live my life."

"I know. And I swear as soon as we get this figured out you will."

"So…why do you think I've been targeted because of you? It's not like we're together." With the exception of the night he'd stayed over, they'd never dated. And they sure weren't dating now.

"It doesn't matter. You are the first woman I've shown interest in...in forever. People who would want to hurt me would use you to do that. I should have seen this coming." There was so much recrimination in his voice.

"Did you used to work for the CIA or something, like Nova?"

"Not exactly. But I do kill people for a living."

CHAPTER TWELVE

—Layla isn't here right now, please leave a message at the beep.—

Xavier watched Layla closely, half expecting her to bolt. As she sat there staring at him, too many emotions flickering across her expressive, beautiful face, he wanted to reach out and comfort her. To make this better.

She continued to sit there, quiet—almost too quiet—then... "I need more details than this."

He started to answer, then heard the ring tone for his grandmother. He cursed. "It's my abuela. I have to answer this."

Her eyes narrowed as he pulled out his cell phone, but she nodded and slid out of the vehicle.

"How is everything?" he asked immediately, watching as Layla headed for the door leading to the mudroom. He quickly typed in the alarm code on his phone app to turn it off just as she stepped inside.

"This home is gorgeous," his grandmother said. "And the man you have keeping an eye on the place is also gorgeous."

He groaned. "Don't tell me that."

"I'm just stating a fact. Now tell me what's going on."

The demand was absolutely fair, considering he'd had his entire family uprooted from Orlando and moved to a safe house in north Florida with zero notice. He hated that he was disrupting his family's life, especially his young cousins. They had school and friends. But there was no way around it. Someone had been looking into Layla and him—and that included his family. They were all in danger until he could figure things out.

"I don't know anything with a hundred percent certainty at this point, but it appears someone wants to hurt me. I could be wrong, and this could have nothing to do with me, but it appears someone targeted Layla because of me. Again, it could be random, but so far the signs say otherwise."

"That sweet girl, is she okay?"

"She's doing...fine." Pissed as hell at him, and he didn't blame her.

"Are you going to tell her what you do for a living?"

"I don't even know how to answer that." Because his own abuela didn't know exactly what he did either. Although who was he kidding, she probably knew exactly what he did. "And I've already told her. Sort of."

There was a beat of silence. "Well? What happened?"

"Nothing. You called after I told her, so I answered."

His grandmother made a frustrated sound then said, "Go talk to her." The line went dead.

Which seemed about right. But he was a giant coward.

Inside, he found Layla in the sterile living room. Something he wouldn't have cared about if it had just been him here.

"I'm surprised your security system wasn't armed," she said, staring at the giant collage he'd created on a white board. It was made up of the faces of people he'd killed combined with other pertinent facts about their lives.

"I disarmed it from my phone when we pulled into the garage."

"Oh. So what is this?"

He came to stand close to her, but kept a foot of space between them. "Gage is working on figuring out who might be targeting me. Or you. And I've broken it down for myself with visuals. I'm handy enough with computers." He had to be, considering his line of work. "But it's easier for me to think and focus with something like this." He'd created two columns on the board. One was of people he'd killed as contract work for the government and the other was independent work—assholes he had no regrets killing. He'd made little notes of relatives or spouses connected to them and who he thought might be a potential threat, but he hadn't made actual labels that said *kills*.

"You've killed all these people." There was no recrimination in her voice. There was no emotion. It was more of a statement than a question.

"Yes." When she didn't respond, he continued even though he'd originally told himself not to make an excuse for what he did. The worse she thought of him the better. Because after this she needed to stay away from him. But he couldn't stand the thought of her recrimination. "On the left are official jobs. Something I shouldn't be telling you."

She shot him a sideways glance and rolled her eyes. "Who am I going to tell?"

It wasn't really a matter of who she would tell but her having the information at all. "I don't like you having this information for various reasons. But right now, that's something we can't worry about. The column on the right is independent jobs I've taken."

Her lip curled up slightly as she looked at the images. "I recognize some of these men. They were not good people."

He scanned the pictures, feeling nothing but relief as he looked at the now dead men. A serial rapist who got out of jail time because of daddy's money, someone who'd run an infamous website that had ruined thousands of lives—he'd also been a serial rapist—and so many others even worse. The world was a better place without them. "I'm not good either. But I have absolutely no guilt or regret for what I've done. Every single person on this board deserved what was coming to them. A hell of a lot sooner than when I killed them."

"Who is your biggest concern here? This guy?" She pointed to the picture in the middle.

"Yes. Or he was. I killed him about six months ago. He was a nasty piece of shit. So was his brother. Diego and Bruno Gomez. They ran drugs and people on the

West Coast. And his brother had been part of my original target as well. But I couldn't get them together. Diego was recently killed by a rival drug runner. Otherwise I would've said this was who was coming after me. He liked to get his hands dirty personally and it's highly likely he would have come after you and me himself. He liked to make his victims suffer."

She looked at him again. "Victims?"

"Yes."

"You feel like expanding on that?"

"No. I'm not giving you visuals that will haunt you forever." He'd retained enough of those to last several lifetimes and he wasn't going to burden her with the sick crimes of these two brothers or anyone else. They were dead now and good riddance. "He liked to hurt women. They both did. At the same time. They were monsters." They'd string women up and... *Ah, hell. Nope.* He had to push the thought out of his mind or she'd see the rage in his eyes. Right now he needed to keep his cool and make her feel as at ease as possible. Safe. Because he was going to keep Layla safe. Or die trying.

"Okay, so not this guy," she said, turning away from him and the board. "So what's the next step?"

"We get a few hours of sleep, then in the morning you and I head out. We're going somewhere even your friends don't know about. You can stay in contact with Nova, but the less they know the better."

Her stare was cool. "I trust Nova with my life. I trust her more than anybody on this planet."

"I know. I'm just trying to keep this circle very small right now. At least until I get you somewhere safe. Gage told me that in addition to someone digging into my background and yours, someone has been looking into my aunt's information as well."

Layla ran a hand over her face, looking exhausted. "I need sleep before I agree to anything. If I go anywhere with you, I'm getting some things from my house first."

"No. Absolutely not."

"I wasn't asking for permission. Unless you're kidnapping me, I'll do what I want. I have very few things in this world that I value, and if we're leaving for however long, I'm taking those things with me." She crossed her arms over her chest, looking fierce and determined.

"I can have someone get them for you."

"We'll see. Do you have any food here?"

Jarred by the abrupt change in topic, he nodded. "I've got a few meals we can microwave." Suddenly he felt totally pathetic for having only that to offer her. "Do you want to talk about anything I told you?" he asked as they headed to the state-of-the-art, yet mostly bare kitchen. White cabinets, white marble countertops, clean lines and all stainless steel appliances that had seen minimal use. There was no life here.

"I'm still trying to wrap my head around all of this," she said, eyeing the kitchen. "And I'm also incredibly angry at you for a lot of things. Mainly for the way you treated me."

"I'm sorry, Layla," he said, meaning it and wishing he could give her more. Wishing he was more. "I left because I thought I was doing the right thing."

She snorted derisively. "The right thing? Please. I'm not even having this conversation with you right now. I don't want to say something I'll regret. Because I have an incredibly strong urge to punch you in the face." She stopped, spun toward him. "You know what? I changed my mind. I'm not hungry. Which room is mine?"

"Upstairs, second door on the left."

Without another word, she left the room. But he wasn't going to let her go hungry so he prepared her dinner anyway then took it upstairs. He knocked on the door once and left, hoping she would take the offering. He might not be able to give her life back to her just yet, but he could at least feed her and watch over her.

Once they got to a safer location he'd get her more than crappy microwavable meals and make sure she had everything she needed. He'd give her the whole world if he could.

* * *

Feeling almost numb, Layla sank onto the end of the king-size bed. The room was so bland and boring with white walls, light wood furniture, and even the duvet set was all white. It was luxury material, but blah. Like she was in some sort of institution or a hospital. Hell, even hospitals had more color than this.

Not that she cared about the color of the room or lack of it anyway. She was simply trying to adjust to this new reality. And she needed to talk to her best friend with one of the burners Xavier had given her.

Thankfully Nova picked up on the first ring. "Hey."

"So Xavier kills people for a living?"

A slight pause followed. "Yeah. I'm sorry."

"You swear you didn't know this when I first met him?"

"Of course not. I kind of knew he was in gray area work but I didn't suspect that he was in the same profession as Axel. If I had known, I'd have told you. He just never really came up when I was talking with Gage."

"Wait a minute. That's how Axel and Xavier know each other?" So Axel had been a hit man too? She'd process that later.

"Oops. Uh, yeah. How are you handling it?"

"I'm mentally exhausted. He thinks we need to go to a safe house. Well, one other than this sad panda house that we're in." It was like he'd gone out of his way to not add any personal touches.

"His place is a dump? He promised that it was safe! He was so—"

"No, it's nice. It's just sad inside. It's like where dreams come to die. Or commit suicide."

Nova snort-giggled at that. "He sounded kind of pathetic when talking to Gage. How are things between you?"

"I don't know. I literally don't know anything at this point other than what he's told me. I know what you said before but…is it really realistic to think someone would target me to get to him?"

"Yes. Gage is rarely wrong. And he doesn't like what he's been finding. Someone has been digging into your records and they've been very careful about it, making sure they cover their tracks. But no one is good enough to outsmart Gage," Nova tacked on, pride in her voice. "The fact that they're trying to cover their tracks is what really bothers him. So yes, I think it's smart of you to lie low with Xavier for a little while. But if you're truly uncomfortable going anywhere with him, we'll work something else out. The crew will easily find another safe house for you and—"

"No, I'm good here." She didn't want to put Nova and the others out any more. After what had happened last year she was starting to feel like a magnet for bad things and she didn't want to become a burden to her best friend. "He's…fine. I can survive staying in a safe house with him." She would just have to forget the attraction and amazing orgasms that Xavier had given her. Or try to downplay them in her mind.

"I'm sorry you're dealing with this shit. Especially after everything you've already been through."

"It's—"

"Don't say fine. It's not fine. It sucks and it's okay to admit it."

She let out a short laugh. "Okay, good call. None of this is anywhere close to fine. But I can deal with this. I need to call the school and cancel out my substitute teaching this week. I feel like a jerk doing it when they already need a substitute in the first place." But that was the least of her worries. She paused as she heard a soft knock on her door.

"Look, I'm going to get some sleep," she said quickly. "But I'll call you tomorrow whenever I figure out what we're going to do, okay?"

"Okay. But don't feel like you're locked into anything with him. If you want to stay here, you will. You have options."

"Okay," she said even though she had no intention of doing any such thing. If even a quarter of what Xavier had told her was true about his enemies, she wasn't going to bring them to her best friend's doorstep.

Once they disconnected she opened the door, and instead of Xavier she found a little tray, with a microwavable meal that was as sad as this house sitting on it. There was also a glass of red wine in a beautifully crafted glass and a napkin folded into a neat little origami design with the silverware tucked inside.

The sight of the little personal touch made her smile despite herself. She was so angry at him and hated what was happening in her life but she couldn't hate him. Because she still cared about him deeply. And she was pretty sure he believed he'd been doing the right thing when he'd ghosted on her.

God, had the man ever been in a relationship before? From what she'd seen, she wasn't so sure he had. She wasn't going to give him a pass for his poor behavior but she might give him a break because, well, she didn't have the energy to stay a ball of rage long term.

And that was all she was going to think about on that subject right now. She was going to eat this crappy food and get some sleep. Because who knew what tomorrow would bring.

CHAPTER THIRTEEN

—What doesn't kill you fucks you up mentally.—

"We are *not* going by your house," Xavier said.

Layla crossed her arms over her chest and sat on the butter-smooth leather couch in the living room. "Then I'm not going anywhere with you."

"Whatever it is you need, we can buy. I have a shit-load of money." There was a little tic in his jaw, but even without it, the frustration on his face was clear. His dark green eyes flared with annoyance.

She told herself not to find that sexy. "You can't buy this."

"Fine. I'll send someone else to get it."

"You said my place was under surveillance. That there were cameras you could check." She'd known that Gage had set them up at Nova's house ages ago, and Xavier had confirmed it by telling her that he was able to monitor her place.

He seemed to fight for patience. "What is it you need?"

"It's a snow globe." One of her most precious possessions, as ridiculous as it sounded.

He blinked, clearly surprised. "I'll buy you a hundred snow globes. A thousand. Anything you want. But I want to get on the road and get away from here now. It'll be easier for me to focus once I've got you holed up somewhere safe."

"I thought you said this place was safe," she said, feeling only a little obnoxious for needling him.

"It is safe. I meant safer." He let out a low growl of frustration and turned away from her. His back was broad, the muscles bunched tight beneath the fabric of his long-sleeved T-shirt.

"The snow globe has sentimental value to me. So if we can't pick it up, you can call someone we trust to pick it up for me. It's on the left little side table in my bedroom."

When he turned back to her, he looked as if his head was about to explode but he simply nodded and pulled out one of his burner phones. Less than two minutes later, he hung up on who she assumed was Axel, given the one-sided conversation she'd heard. "It's done."

She smiled sweetly and stood, feeling completely obnoxious by this point and not caring. "Thank you."

"So what's up with this snow globe? Was it a gift from…an ex?" She was surprised by his surly tone.

He had no right to be moody or anything. She was in this stupid mess potentially because of him and she was feeling more than annoyed this morning. She'd barely slept and she was heading into the unknown again. "Why would it matter?"

He didn't respond, simply turned and headed up the stairs.

All right, then.

By the time she was pouring herself a cup of coffee in a to-go tumbler, he returned from upstairs with her little work bag. "I wasn't kidding when I said I'll buy you whatever you want. Clothes, shoes, entertainment, anything."

"Thank you," she said, securing the top on the tumbler. But money couldn't buy what she wanted. It couldn't buy safety or fix her life, and it couldn't make things between them the way she wanted. The way they'd been before. "Did you want me to fix you a cup as well?" At this point, she was going to be civil with him. She wasn't sure how long they were going to be together, and even if she was feeling cranky, she didn't need to have a bad attitude. That would just make them both miserable and everything would feel that much more awful. It was time to suck things up.

"I've got it, but thank you." His tone was softer now, and the way he looked at her with those warm eyes... *Dammit.*

Once they were on the road, she said, "Before I lived with Nova in foster care, before Ms. Baker, I lived with a woman in her thirties. Ms. Isabella Wilson. I was her first and only foster kid. She worked at a local food bank and I guess she knew my mom. Or had seen her around— they weren't friends or anything."

She nearly snorted at that.

"She was always sneaking me little treats, and I'm the reason she ended up applying to become a foster parent. I was lucky enough to live with her for a little while after my mom overdosed. She wanted to adopt me. But then she was diagnosed with terminal cancer. And since she had shitty healthcare..." Layla cleared her throat, shoving back the swell of emotions as she thought about how different her life could have been, about the loss of one of the kindest women she'd ever known. "Anyway, she gave me a snow globe and told me to follow my dreams. To never let anyone tell me I didn't matter or wasn't worthy."

Xavier was silent for a long moment as he drove through the city streets. "Hell. If you'd told me that earlier, I would've picked up the damn thing myself," he murmured, making her smile.

"I know it's just a thing. But it matters to me. It's the only thing I've held on to from my childhood. When you're in the system you live out of a suitcase, and that was always the thing I took with me wherever I went." It was a miracle the snow globe was still in one piece. After what had happened with her ex, the Feds had actually retrieved it for her from his house.

He scrubbed a hand over his face. "I'm sorry."

"What are you sorry for?"

"I'm just sorry in general. Sorry you had a shitty childhood. Sorry that your ex was who he was. And I'm sorry you're stuck in this situation with me for the foreseeable future."

She looked out the window away from him. "You don't have to be sorry about the third thing. I'm still angry at you but I know you don't want to be in this situation any more than I do."

He was silent as she watched the city go by and that was answer enough. He didn't want to be here with her.

"Shit," Xavier muttered, pulling her out of her thoughts. "Brace!"

She'd snapped her head around to look at him, ready to ask him what he meant, when a truck rammed into them, slamming into the left back side.

Metal crunched and tires squealed as they went into a tailspin. Her body jerked against the seat belt, pinning her in place.

Heart in her throat, Layla clutched at the center console and side of the door as they spun wildly.

Xavier held on to the wheel, adjusting it quickly before righting it. She wasn't sure why the airbags hadn't deployed but shelved that for later. "Xavier—"

"Not an accident," he snapped, his knuckles white against the steering wheel.

Oh God. She turned around to look out the back window and spotted an SUV racing after them. The truck that had hit them was haphazardly parked on a sidewalk but the SUV was gaining speed. "Should I call the police?" She pulled out one of her burner phones. There were two vehicles involved in this mess, and one had given chase—clearly they needed backup now.

"Don't bother," he said, taking a sharp turn down a side street filled with shops.

She wanted to ask why not but held her tongue. He had more experience in situations like this. Or she assumed he did.

"Should I call Nova or Gage?" She turned around again. The SUV was still behind them. Ice sliced through her veins. They were being hunted and he was all calm.

If he could keep his shit together, so could she. For now. She hoped.

"Nope." He took a left turn. Then a right. Then left.

The SUV remained on their tail. It didn't matter how fast Xavier went or how much he maneuvered, the SUV never lost them.

"What are we going to do?" Panic punched through her and she was unable to hide the pop of fear in her tone.

"I'm going to stop them." His tone was insanely calm, making her feel nominally better. He seemed to be in control, to know exactly what he was doing.

Internally she felt like a can of wasps had been released and she was running around screaming in stark terror—but on the outside, she managed to keep it together.

She felt helpless as he made another sharp turn and sped toward a group of warehouses. She wasn't familiar enough with Redemption Harbor but she knew they were close to the water now. One of the warehouses had a bunch of old-looking boats inside it but the rest of the doors were closed. She hated this feeling, like she was out of control with no way to protect herself.

"I'm going to need some words from you right now," she finally said. "What the hell are you going to do about these guys?"

To her annoyance, he simply reached into his center console and pulled out a remote control. When he pressed the button, the door to the closest warehouse started rolling up. They were maybe thirty yards from it now. What the hell?

He tossed the remote down and snapped the console shut. Still driving, he reached down and pulled out a small pistol he handed to her. "This is for you if things go south."

Layla glanced behind them. The SUV was barreling down on them now that they weren't around any witnesses. Why the hell had he brought them here? At least on the main street they'd been in a public enough place.

She wanted to tell him no but she took the pistol even though it went against her instincts. Thanks to Skye she at least knew how to use the thing.

"This vehicle is bullet resistant. But it won't withstand an RPG," he said, zooming through the open warehouse door.

"An RPG?" she blurted. Was he freaking kidding her?

As the SUV barreled in after them, Xavier threw the vehicle into park and hit the remote again. The door started shutting, enclosing the other vehicle inside with them. Trapping them together. Then he reached under his seat again and to her surprise, rolled down his window—and tossed out two silver canisters.

Gas started filling the warehouse immediately.

"You just have that stuff in your vehicle?"

"Always be prepared," he murmured. "A good motto to live by."

She stared at him for a long second, realizing she didn't know him. She might be wildly attracted to him and they might have shared a friendship over the last few months, but she didn't know the real him. Or she wasn't sure she could. Maybe she knew a small part of him, but all this? This was a side to Xavier she hadn't imagined.

He jumped into the middle seat and reached over into the far back seat. Then he tossed a gas mask to her.

"Put it on," he said, even as he started putting on his own.

Holy shit, this was her life now. She was putting on a gas mask because the man she was with had tossed out a couple smoke grenades. Shaking her head, she did as he'd instructed and slid it on over her head. The thing was bulky and foreign to her. Before she could try to tighten it, he was right next to her making sure it fit properly. How many of these things did he have back there?

She noticed he also had multiple weapons. A gun with a silencer in his hand and two visible guns tucked into a holster under his jacket. Considering the smoke grenades and RPG reference earlier, she guessed he had more tucked away.

With his hands he motioned that she should follow him. As he opened the door, he tossed out another canister, then grabbed her hand. Smoke billowed everywhere, making it almost impossible to see.

"Don't let go of me," he said, his voice muffled. Or she thought that was what he said.

No way in hell was she letting go of him. The gas mask made it difficult to see anywhere other than directly in front of her but Xavier seemed to know *exactly* what he was doing. His movements were sharp and precise.

She clutched his hand tight, barely able to see a foot in front of her. Her heart was a wild, staccato beat in her chest, the sound almost louder than her Darth Vader-style breathing in this stupid mask.

Ping. Ping. Ping.

Holy shit, someone was shooting at the SUV. Even if the shooters couldn't see, they might get lucky and hit *them.*

Her heart rate kicked up a billion notches as she silently hurried along with Xavier, holding his forearm in a death grip.

His strides were steady and he didn't bother shooting back. It belatedly registered that he likely wasn't shooting because if he did it would give away their location.

She jumped, her grip tightening on Xavier when she heard a clicking sound. But suddenly a door opened in front of them. No longer was smoke billowing around them like something out of a Halloween carnival house.

Xavier had led them to a back exit.

As they stepped outside, he pulled a small detonator-type thing out of his jacket pocket, then pressed another button.

The building walls shook ominously as he ripped off his gas mask. Just as quickly he loosened then pulled off hers.

She sucked in a sharp breath, inhaling the crisp air.

"Are you okay?" he asked, scanning her in a purely clinical fashion.

"I'm fine." She was shaky but okay. If she'd been shot earlier, he sure as hell would've known. Everyone would've known.

She had so many questions, like what had just blown up or why did he carry around canisters of gas. Although the answer seemed pretty obvious. *Because he's very likely to need them.* Duh. Her brain was just sluggish right now as she tried to adjust to this crazy reality.

"What do we do now?"

"Come on, you can't stay out here in the open. Head over there to the warehouse. The code on the back door is three, six, eight, nine, seven. Can you remember that?"

"You own that warehouse?" she asked dumbly.

"Layla, focus."

She mentally shook herself and realized that tension was rolling off him. She needed to move so she repeated the numbers back to him.

"Good. Go inside. There's an office door to the left. Go inside there and barricade yourself. It's the equivalent of a safe room. Same code for that door. Go."

Oh God. But she didn't dare argue. "Be safe," she said. There was more she wanted to say to him but now clearly wasn't the time. They just needed to stay alive.

* * *

Xavier watched as Layla disappeared behind the other warehouse exit door. He wasn't sure how either of them had been tracked but he would figure it out as soon as he got his questions answered.

Weapon out, he slipped back in the way he'd come. The smoke from his grenades was already dissipating, but the crumbling mass of his SUV was contributing even more.

Soon enough someone would call the cops if they hadn't already.

He'd picked the warehouses in this area specifically— because of the back exit getaway and because it was far enough away from the local PD so he should have some time. He had a plan everywhere he stayed or temporarily lived. He refused to be caged or go to jail.

And he went out of his way to ensure that would never happen.

As he quietly made his way around the edge of the warehouse, he heard groaning. Good. He'd most likely injured one or both of his attackers.

Ignoring the sounds of pain, he continued creeping around the outer edge of the warehouse, looking for any signs of movement among the billowing smoke and gas. He hated wearing gas masks, but in his line of work having this backup was a necessity.

There. A flash of movement shifting across the concrete floor.

Though he was taking a risk, he saw one guy lying flat on his back, half his face blown off, and another guy crawling toward the wounded one. There could be more operators nearby but he was playing the odds that it was just two of them. Because he didn't like leaving Layla alone longer than necessary. Even now, he hated being away from her. Hated not having eyes on her and knowing she was safe.

His shoes were silent as he raced over to the two men. He shot the injured man twice in the chest with practiced efficiency, putting him out of his misery.

The crawling man let out a sharp sound and swiveled, bringing up a weapon as he did. But his movements were sluggish.

It clattered across the floor as Xavier kicked it out of his hand. Then he slammed his boot into the man's chest. Not hard enough to crack ribs. Not yet. He needed this guy to talk first. He would have no mercy for these men who had wanted to hurt Layla. Who knew what they would have done if they'd gotten their hands on her? He didn't give a fuck about himself but they had put her in danger. Hell, she could have died in the crash if they'd timed it right. And for that they would pay.

The man shot out with his foot, kicking Xavier in the ankle. He stumbled, but got his footing fast, striking out at the man on the ground again.

This time he slammed his boot against the guy's knee. "This is going to end one of two ways," he said as the man screamed in pain. Xavier holstered his weapon even as he grabbed the guy by the front of his shirt and hauled him to his one good leg. "You're going to die," he said. "But it's up to you how much I make you suffer first."

He didn't relish torture. Never had and never would. But he would do what he had to and get his answers.

The man lifted an arm, attempting to lash out at Xavier, but it was weak.

Keeping Layla firmly in the front of his mind, Xavier began his grisly task.

CHAPTER FOURTEEN

—Sometimes you've just got to go with the flow.—

Layla tensed as the door handle to the little office she was in rattled. She had the gun Xavier had given her but she didn't think she could actually shoot anyone. Maybe hit somebody with a bat, yes, but shoot someone?

"It's me!" Xavier called out. A second later, the door flew open. His pale scar pulled taut with his tense expression. "Come on, we've gotta go now."

She jumped up from her crouched position and grabbed the gun. He immediately took it from her and tucked it in one of his many holsters.

"How many people were there?" she asked.

"Two guys."

"They're dead?"

He shot her a sideways glance as he gently took her elbow. "By now someone has called the cops. We've really got to get out of here."

She heard sirens in the distance but for some reason panic wasn't punching through her like it had been before. Probably because she just felt numb at this point. Was this what an out of body experience was like? "How are we going to get out of here?"

"I've got a plan," he said as they stepped out into the intense sunlight. "This way," he said, pointing to a chain-link fence.

"You want to scale that thing?" Curled barbed wire covered the top of it, making it impossible to jump over.

He simply shook his head and took her hand in his. With no choice but to go with him, she hurried across the pavement then the small patch of grass lining the front of the long fence line. That was when she saw that there was a very thin seam bisecting the fence. And she could only see it up close. "Was this already cut?"

"I cut it a month ago."

"You were planning on being attacked like this?" She ducked through the opening when he held open the fence for her.

He followed through after her. "Not this scenario exactly, but anything can happen."

"Are you okay? I mean, did those guys hurt you?" Something she probably should have asked earlier, but come on, she was barely keeping it together.

He simply snorted.

All right, then. She didn't see blood so she assumed he was fine. "I'm glad you're not hurt," she murmured as they made their way through a thicket of underbrush and spindly trees.

He grunted, the sound full of disbelief.

"I *am* glad you're okay. I might be angry at you but that doesn't mean I want you hurt," she snapped, annoyed in general. But seriously annoyed that he actually thought she wouldn't care one way or the other if something happened to him.

He took her hand, squeezed tight. "I'm so sorry you're in this mess. And I'm going to get you out of it."

Looking up into his eyes, she felt that familiar flutter in her belly but she quickly squashed it and glanced away from him. "Let's get out of here." Because the sirens were getting louder in the distance and she wasn't sure how on earth they would explain a blown-up vehicle and two dead guys if they were caught.

* * *

"What are you doing?" Layla asked when Xavier pulled off the highway onto an exit with only one gas station and a McDonald's. He had a full tank of gas and there weren't any cops pulling them over so she wasn't sure what he could be doing.

He'd assured her the older model truck they were in wasn't stolen. And she believed him since he'd had the keys on his person. They'd only had to walk a mile and a half to get to where it had been sitting in the parking lot of a local craft store.

"Ditching everything that's ours."

"What do you mean?"

"Our clothes, all the burner phones, everything. I don't know how we were tracked but we're starting fresh."

"Why don't we just call Nova or any one of her crew?" Surely they would be able to provide valuable backup.

"I seriously don't know how we were tracked," he repeated. "The guy wouldn't tell me."

"You can't think they had anything to do with it?" Rage bubbled up inside her at his insinuation. Nova was the best friend she'd ever had. Her sister, if not by blood. No way would Nova ever betray her.

"Of course not! I just mean I don't know *how* we were tracked. I don't think anyone betrayed us. I'm just trying to be smart so we can get somewhere safe and start over with all new phones and electronics."

"Oh...okay. So what's the plan after this?"

"We go to ground. We find a place we can lie low at. I think I might know who was after you, and if I'm right, this whole situation is definitely related to me."

"Did you know those guys?" she asked, scanning the area surrounding them. It looked so desolate out here. Only a few of the trees had leaves, the ground looked icy and there were two cars in the parking lot of the rundown McDonald's.

"Not personally, but yeah. I know of them."

Well clearly he wasn't going to expand, but she would push him later. "We need to call Nova and let her know—"

"Nope. We're not calling anyone just yet."

Damn it. She'd thought he might have changed his mind. "She's going to be worried about me."

"I texted Gage, told him we're going dark."

Layla gritted her teeth. That would have to do, even if she didn't like it. And truthfully, she thought he might be right. Maybe they should cut contact with everyone for the near future. That would keep her friends out of danger, hopefully.

"I've got clothes for you," he said. "Well, they're mine, so they'll be too big but you can wear them for now."

She couldn't imagine that her clothing had been marked or whatever, but since this wasn't a hill she was going to die on, she gave in. "Fine." Still, she didn't care if he'd seen her naked before—he wasn't going to now. "I'll jump in the back and change. And you better not peek."

"Promise." Despite the situation, his lips quirked up ever so slightly and she was under the impression he was trying not to smile.

CHAPTER FIFTEEN

—Bad ideas are my specialty.—

"I don't like this," Nova said for the tenth time. She pushed up from her seat at the conference table where she was gathered around with the whole crew. She wasn't always part of the round table discussions, but considering her best friend was the one in danger, she was going to be involved with anything to do with Layla right now. This was like last year all over. Okay, maybe not exactly like what had happened before, but her best friend was in danger again and it made Nova crazy.

"Well Xavier went completely off the grid after he texted me so there's not much we can do about it right now." Gage was somehow unperturbed by all this.

"But you're my super-hacker. Why can't you find them?"

"Because he ditched all their phones and I don't know what he's driving. Technically I could run Xavier and Layla's faces through a facial recognition software database but Xavier is careful. I don't think it would help right now, and if someone else is locked into one of the systems, it might alert them that they've gone off grid. Unless you want me to start hacking satellites?" he asked, completely serious. "I will find them if you want."

"No," she grumbled.

"Good. Because I've got other things to discuss right now. Which is why I called this meeting," he said pointedly.

"When do we start kicking ass?" Skye asked from the end of the table. But she wasn't sitting in a chair around the conference table like everyone else. Instead she sat on the actual table at the very end, cross-legged with C-4 snoozing in her lap. Colt and Axel were sitting on one side of her, with Brooks and Savage on the other. And Savage kept throwing pistachios at Brooks, who was somehow completely unperturbed by his friend's antics.

They definitely weren't big on formality around here. Thank God for that. Nova had worked in an office before. More than one. Never again. She couldn't imagine going back to her former life now. Even if she felt like pulling her hair out with worry at the moment.

"If you guys would stop talking," Gage said, some of the irritation starting to show, "I could tell you. After Xavier's text, I got a hit on two dead guys nearby. Heard about it on the local PD frequency. Apparently these two guys were both shot at point-blank range—once in the head and twice in the chest—in a warehouse owned by someone who does not exist. The cops don't know that part yet, but I figured it out.

"Anyway, in addition to the dead guys, there was an SUV left smoldering from a pre-wired explosion—I hacked the PD in case that's not clear by now, and that was in the report. And there were a few empty smoke grenade canisters left behind. I'm still trying to figure out who owns that warehouse but I'm pretty sure it's Xavier.

And I'll tell you why later, before one of you asks," he said sharply, because they always interrupted him. "First, we're going to talk about the dead guys because they're important. The men are Brant Clark and Calvin Long. They're linked fairly closely with the Murphy brothers, who, as you know, are on Xavier's suspect list." He motioned to the wall where he'd set up an array of various screens for their viewing. Images of Adam and Steve Murphy popped up along with their very long dossier. "Xavier killed their older brother. Dude deserved it too. This was off the books work he did as well. So not CIA-related."

"Where are the Murphy brothers right now?" Skye asked.

"Still trying to narrow down a location," Gage said. "As of right now they're close to Redemption Harbor. They're being careful to cover their tracks, but not careful enough."

"This has to be why Xavier and Layla went dark," Nova said. "These guys must have tried to hurt her or Xavier."

Gage nodded once, and she knew her fiancé well enough to realize he was holding something back. "What?" she asked.

"I found some CCTV footage that showed these guys chasing after an SUV I'm pretty sure was Xavier's. I couldn't see who was in the SUV so there must have been a protective film on the windows. Which makes me think it was definitely Xavier's."

"I wish he'd told you more." More than that, Nova wished she could talk to Layla, to hear her voice and know she was okay. Because right about now she was dealing with a whole lot of guilt because she should have insisted Layla stay with her. But she'd thought Layla would be better off with Xavier. Those two had a whole lot of unfinished business, and despite what her friend told her, Nova was pretty sure Layla had fallen hard for the man. She'd wanted them to have a chance at what she had with Gage. Maybe that had been a mistake.

Gage lifted a shoulder. "Me too."

"Quit beating yourself up," Skye said, tossing a piece of caramel popcorn in her mouth. C-4 stirred slightly, looked up at her owner, then went back to sleeping. Lazy dog.

Nova frowned at her. "Are you talking to me?"

"Yes," her friend said. "I can see the wheels turning in your head right now. Layla is fine. Xavier will keep her safe. We all talked about it. He would literally take a bullet for her and he won't be distracted—she's his number one priority. Her being with him is a *good* thing."

"It would still be better if I could talk to her," Nova muttered.

"Agreed. But you can't, so focus on what you can do for her." Skye turned back to Gage. "So right now our main suspects are the brothers. What can we do to ferret these guys out?" she asked.

At that, the whole team started talking, discussing ways to bring these guys out into the open.

Nova listened, but her mind was on her best friend. She really hoped Layla was okay right now. Because if anything happened to her, Nova would never forgive herself.

* * *

Layla opened her eyes with a start, momentarily disoriented by how quiet it was.

She pushed up from the king-sized bed and looked around the large room. Moonlight streamed in from one of the high, triangle-shaped windows in the A-frame house.

She listened for any noise, but didn't hear anything. The two-bedroom house was technically a two-story, but from the road it looked like a one story. She'd seen houses like this before, usually in the mountains. She wasn't sure how Xavier had found this place but he assured her it was safe. They didn't have any neighbors in any direction for miles. He said he liked this place because it would be easy to see an enemy coming from all directions.

Which made her feel better and kind of worse at the same time. Because they were on the run from a faceless ghost who could take them out at any moment. *Ugh.* She glanced over at the little clock on the nightstand. Three in the morning.

She knew herself well enough that she wouldn't go back to sleep now. They'd driven for a few hours yesterday before arriving at this place. They were in North Carolina now and not on the coast.

She opened the bedroom door and saw that the little fireplace was still going in the living room. From her position at the top of the stairs she could see it below but the rest of the house was directly under the huge master suite she'd been in. She couldn't hear anything so she guessed Xavier was still asleep in his own room.

After they'd arrived yesterday, Xavier had gone out to get food for them, then he'd basically retreated to the other bedroom where he'd been doing who knew what on his computer as he tried to hunt down who was after them. Even if she had been angry at him, she missed the closeness between them. Whether she'd really known him at all, she still missed him even as they shared a roof.

As she reached the bottom of the stairs and turned, she saw Xavier at the square dining room table working on his laptop. The place was open concept so the kitchen and dining area all flowed together right off the living room. He looked up at her and half-smiled, the thin pale line across his right cheek standing out under the light.

She felt the jolt of that little look all the way to her core. Feeling oddly self-conscious in his baggy clothes, she made her way to the little dining room area where he sat with papers spread out in front of his laptop under the big chandelier made out of faux deer antlers.

"How long have you been up?" He had a half-empty mug of coffee next to him.

"Since about midnight."

"Do you think you should get some sleep?" she asked, sitting down next to him. The wood floor was cool against her bare feet.

"I can't turn my brain off," he murmured, leaning back in the chair now. He wore a simple black T-shirt that stretched across his muscular chest. What was it with him and those shirts? It was like he wore them to torment her.

She had a sudden flash of what it had been like to kiss and stroke that chest. To clutch onto his arms as they'd made out like teenagers. Feeling her cheeks heat up, she abruptly stood and hurried to the attached kitchen area. She wanted him but she wasn't so sure she should at this point.

The kitchen was decorated in what she imagined was standard mountain-style decor. Red and black plaid curtains with little black bears dotting them hung over the small, square window. A pendant lamp hanging down over the sink had a bear and mountain scene silhouetted against beveled glass. The hand towels had moose and bears on them, and even the paper towel holder had a black bear and mountain scene around the bottom of it.

She wasn't going back to sleep for a long while so she poured herself a cup of coffee—in a green mug that had yet another black bear on it. Feeling more under control, she went to sit back at the table with Xavier who had been intently watching her.

"Is there anything I can do to help?" she asked.

"If there was, I would tell you," he said, his tone soft. "At this point I'm basically running various programs, and they're automated. I'm pretty much banging my head against a wall trying to see if there's something I missed. But I heard from Gage—"

"You did?" She straightened in her chair, wrapping her fingers tightly around her warm mug.

"Yeah. We're talking on a secure channel. No phones. And we're keeping our conversations limited. I'm glad I reached out because he's come up with the same information I have—more, even, because that guy is talented. We both think it's these two midlevel gunrunners who are after me. The Murphy brothers."

She recognized the name Murphy from his white board from before. A name was a good thing. If they had a name, they could stop them. "Do you know where they are?"

"Gage says they're outside Redemption Harbor." He ran a hand over his face and for the first time she saw the stress lines bracketing his mouth. So maybe he wasn't as cool about all this as she'd thought.

She had the urge to reach out and comfort him, to curl up against him and kiss that stress away. "That's good, right?"

He nodded once. "It's definitely better that we know who this threat is."

"Can I ask you something personal?" she asked. "Only if it's not going to take you away from what you're doing."

Sighing, he shut his laptop. "I need to clear my head anyway. I'm just spinning my wheels now. Ask whatever you want." He pinned her with those dark green eyes, making her shift slightly in her seat.

She could easily lose herself in his eyes. But not now. Not yet. Maybe never again. Layla wondered if she was opening up a can of worms but she didn't really care at this point. She wanted to know more about him. The real him. The one he'd kept hidden from her over the course of their friendship. "Why did you get into your current profession? Or how...or both, I guess."

His expression didn't change but he went still in that sort of preternatural way she noticed about him sometimes. "Are you sure you want to know all this?" he asked. Before she could answer, he let out a harsh breath. "Of course you're sure. Sorry, I'm just stalling. The way I got into this line of work kind of goes back to when I was a teenager."

Her shocked expression must've been clear even though she tried to hide it because he gave a half-smile. "I don't mean I started when I was a teenager. I just mean I need to tell you a little bit more about who I was when I was younger to explain how I ended up where I have."

"Okay." She braced herself for the rest.

He hesitated a moment longer. "When I was about thirteen, my parents died. Which you already know. What I didn't tell you before is that it was a dark time for me. My grandmother and aunts took me in and they were more than happy to. They loved me unconditionally, gave me all the love I could have wanted. But I was angry and an ungrateful little shit. I was angry at the world and I fell in with the wrong crowd. And honestly I might've fallen in with them even if my parents hadn't died, so that's just an excuse. I thought I was hot shit and wanted to prove to myself, and the world I guess, that I was tough so...I joined a gang."

She tried to keep her expression neutral but it still surprised her. That wasn't the vibe she'd gotten from him at all. And he had a few tattoos, but they were all from the Marine Corps.

He gave her a wry smile. "I wasn't always the law-abiding citizen you see before you," he said, his tone tinged with sarcasm. "Anyway. I got into a lot of trouble. I was on a bad path, and a judge told me to join the military or I'd end up in prison soon—and then he was certain I'd end up dead. He said he didn't want to see that happen. And honest to God, I think that judge actually cared. My abuela told me exactly what I was going to do and for the first time in years I listened to her. I'd been such a disappointment to her that I knew I had to make things right.

"So I joined the Marines and they turned me into a weapon basically. But it gave me the structure I needed— the true friendships I'd been lacking. I loved every moment of being in the Corps. Even when I didn't realize I loved it, I did. It's where I met Axel and a few others I'm a better man for knowing. When I got out I was more or less recruited by the CIA. Not directly but as a contract worker. I don't always accept contracts from them though. I've always been able to pick and choose. After a while I realized that I could take contracts on my own, so I did. As far as your other question, the why of what I do...it's because I'm good at it and I've made a lot of money. I was able to move my whole family up to Orlando to a safe, quiet, gated neighborhood. They all have good lives, and with the exception of right now with them being in hiding because of me, they've remained untouched by my sins. And my sins are something I can very much live with because the people I've put under the dirt deserve to be there."

There was so much recrimination in his voice, she couldn't help herself—she reached her hand across the little table and took his hand in hers. "Have you ever killed..."

He shifted slightly against his chair, his brows drawing together. "What?"

She didn't say anything, unsure how much she wanted to know about him.

"What...like, kids?" he practically barked. "No!" He snapped his hand away from hers, as if burned, but then slowly slid it back onto the table, gently touching his fingertips to hers. "I have certain guidelines I follow. The people I target have crossed certain lines in society that aren't acceptable. Hell, if you want me to be blunt, they're all monsters who have no respect for their fellow man. Now you see why we can't be together?"

She was silent for a long moment, but she didn't pull her hand away. "You mean because of your enemies? Or because you've killed people?"

"Both. I've already brought a threat to your doorstep. I should have left Redemption Harbor ages ago."

"Why did you stay?" Now that she knew what his job truly was, he could have lived anywhere.

He gave her a pointed look, and she felt the weight of his stare all the way to her toes. "I think that's obvious."

"I want to hear why." At this point she was pretty sure he meant because of her but she still wanted to hear the words. She needed to so she understood what the hell was happening between them.

He leaned forward on the table, pushing into her personal space. "Because of you. Because I can't get you out of my head. I've never wanted another woman the way I want you. And it's more than just want. I...like everything about you, Layla. But..." His shoulders bunched up as he sat back. "It's not to be."

"Says who? You?" She was still wrapping her head around what he'd told her but she'd realized a couple things as he talked. There were definitely some things she could live with. And as weird as it sounded even in her own head, she could live with what he'd done. But only if he quit now.

"Yes, says me. You heard everything I said," he growled. "I will do nothing but bring you pain."

"I don't know, you brought me a lot of pleasure the other night." The words just slipped out.

His eyes widened. She'd clearly shocked him, something she didn't think she'd ever done before. He opened his mouth once then snapped it shut before abruptly standing. He picked up his coffee mug and strode into the kitchen where he methodically washed it and set it on the drying rack. "Are you hungry? I can make us breakfast." His tone was tight, too controlled to come off as natural.

As she watched him move, a low heat stirred in her belly. Seriously, she must have brain damage because what he'd told her should have warned her off. She was still hurt by the way he'd ghosted on her but it made more sense now. Way more sense.

Xavier didn't seem to think he deserved any sort of relationship, and he'd been willing to put aside his own happiness because he thought it would keep her safe. He wanted to protect her from everything, including from himself. How could she not be moved by that?

Picking up her own mug, she followed him into the little kitchen and set it in the sink as he opened the re-frigerator door, studiously ignoring meeting her eye. "Xavier, look at me please."

Sighing, he shut the door and turned to look at her. Then he shoved his hands in his jogging pants pockets, looking unsure of himself for the first time since she'd met him. It didn't do anything to take away from the mouthwatering sexiness he exuded.

"Is what you told me the only reason you ghosted on me? It wasn't because you changed your mind about...your attraction to me?"

He stepped forward, letting his hands fall to the side. "I left because I never want to see you hurt or in danger."

"Well it's a little too late for the danger part." She took a step closer, and given the small square footage of the kitchen, ended up right in front of him. Taking a chance, she tentatively laid her fingertips against his warm, unfortunately covered chest.

He closed his eyes, letting out a long breath at her touch, but he didn't pull back. If anything, he seemed to lean into her. "Layla, we can't..."

Stepping forward fully, she pulled him into a hug, setting her cheek on his chest. She needed the contact right now. Hell, she needed Xavier, and only his touch.

"You did hurt me, but now it makes more sense," she said as she stared at the stainless steel refrigerator. It was easier to talk to him without looking into his face. "And I'm not angry at you anymore."

His grip around her tightened and there was no hiding his erection pressing against her abdomen. Thick and heavy. "You can't say that," he rasped out.

"Why not?"

"It's better if you hate me."

She pulled back slightly but kept her arms around him. The need to touch him was overwhelming. Especially since she'd already had a taste. She wanted all she could get. "I don't hate you. I never did."

"We can't do anything right now, Layla. You're in danger just by being near me." He set his hands on her hips, his fingers flexing possessively before he dropped his hold. But he still didn't back up.

"I'm in danger whether we do anything or not," she whispered.

He shook his head once, his lips a tight line. "We can't have a future. Even if we—once we get out of this mess, I can't put you in danger again."

She understood that, she really did. "Why can't we be together right now? At least until everything is over?" She wanted more, but she would take what she could get where he was concerned.

"I...fuck. This is a bad idea," he growled, even as his head descended, his mouth crushing against hers.

Apparently bad ideas were her specialty. She teased her tongue against his, moaning into his mouth as she plastered herself against him. She wanted to experience all of him, no matter what the future held. Because if they didn't survive this, she would regret not holding on to him, not claiming him. However temporary that claiming would be.

CHAPTER SIXTEEN

—I hope your day is as nice as your butt.—

With self-control he didn't know he had, Xavier tore his mouth from Layla's. "We need to stop before this gets out of hand." Words he kept repeating to himself over and over.

And ignoring.

His dick sure as hell wasn't listening to reason.

She tightened her grip on his shoulders. "Why? Because it's for my own good?"

"Once this is over, I have to walk away. I can't offer you everything you deserve," he rasped out. "And you deserve a fucking picket fence, everything you never had growing up. You deserve someone so much better than me. Someone who can stick around. Someone who will treat you like a queen the rest of your life."

She sucked in a little breath. "I'm not asking for a future. I just want right now. Because if we do have to part ways, I want everything from you. I want to treasure those memories." Her amber eyes sparked with heat and something else he was afraid to define.

"I want more for you than someone like me. I'm damaged, Layla." And he didn't deserve her.

Her expression softened. "We're all damaged."

Dammit. She was giving him everything he wanted. Well not everything, because he wanted her forever. He wanted to tell her that too, but he somehow refrained. Because if he said the words, if he admitted that he loved her, he didn't think he could let her go. Hell, he was on a razor-sharp line as it was and he wasn't sure he could walk away regardless.

"You're thinking too much," she murmured even as she stepped back from him. Giving him the space he'd demanded.

She was putting the ball in his court now, he realized. He'd apologized and she had accepted. Not only that, she'd accepted him for who he was. The real him. He'd admitted all of his sins and she was standing in front of him offering herself, and he didn't think he could say no. He was only a man.

A very weak one when it came to Layla. Who was he kidding? He couldn't walk away right now. Later, yes. Because it was necessary. But now? He was rock-hard and obsessed with wondering how she would feel wrapped around him. "If you want to stop, we—"

"I don't want to stop anything," she snapped, all fiery passion.

That was what had first attracted him to her, that combination of her wildness and sweetness. There was fire in her eyes and she had a smart mouth he couldn't get enough of. Not to mention her curves drove him to his knees, made him want to worship at her altar.

He couldn't have any room for regrets. Not now. Not when their future was unknown. Because if he died and he didn't get to claim all of her, he *would* die with regrets. The world was cruel, dangling Layla in front of him, giving him just a taste of her, only for this to be temporary. Well fuck it, he was going to embrace this time with her. He was going to hold on tight for as long as he could.

He crushed his mouth to hers again and hoisted her up against him. She was so perfect, molding to him as if they'd been made for each other. Walking while kissing her, he made it to the small living room. With his foot, he shoved the coffee table out of the way, then grabbed a handful of blankets from the big couch, tossing them onto the thick rug in front of the fireplace. There was no way they were making it to his room or upstairs. He had to taste her now or he felt as if he might die.

She let out a gasp of surprise when he stretched her out on the fluffy blankets but her eyes still simmered with that heat.

Heat and hunger. All for him.

She lifted her hips, a clear invitation for him to take her loose pajama pants off. Once he stripped her completely—moving at warp fucking speed—he sucked in a sharp breath. With the shadows from the firelight flickering off her curvy body, she was everything he remembered and more. Even better this second time around. The taste of her was seared into his brain and he wanted more. Always more when it came to her.

This had to be just about right now, just about the temporary. At least that was what he told himself as he buried his face between her legs, savoring the way she cried out his name, the perfection of her taste. Oh God. *This* was heaven.

She was already wet, arching against his mouth with a cry of pleasure as he flicked his tongue along her slick folds. God, she was so wet, and it was all because of him.

He loved that he turned her on, that she was here with him even now that she knew everything about him. He didn't have to hide who he was from his sweet Layla.

He wasn't sure why the hell she hadn't turned away from him in disgust but he thanked God she hadn't. He had to make her come again. To make her come so hard that she would never forget him when he walked away. He wanted to be etched into her brain forever, even if it made him a selfish bastard.

He held her hips in his hands, keeping her still. She was already under his skin and he wanted to be under hers. Because he would take her with him wherever he went. She would live inside him.

He focused on her clit, savoring the sweet sounds of pleasure she made as she rolled her hips against his face, over and over, completely wild and uninhibited as she dug her fingers into his scalp. The bite of pain had his cock jerking against his pants and he felt as if he could bust right through them.

"Xavier," she moaned. And then she was climaxing, her cries wild as he slid two fingers inside her. Fuck, she was tight.

He felt the little pulses of her around his fingers as she orgasmed, sharp and loud.

He was amped up, all his muscles pulled taut with the need to be inside her. Before he could make a move, she pushed up, breathless and sated-looking.

Taking him by surprise, she playfully shoved at his chest. "On your back," she ordered, her words breathy and heady.

He rolled onto his back, stripping his shirt over his head as he moved. Normally he liked to be in control but he would gladly give up the reins for her.

When she bit her lip, groaning as she raked her gaze over him, he felt like a peacock, puffing his chest out proudly. He kept in shape to stay alive, but he cared what she thought about him and was glad she liked what she saw.

She tugged his pants and boxer briefs off, tossing them in the opposite direction of the fireplace. When she ducked her head between his legs, taking him into her mouth, he completely forgot to breathe as she sucked his cock as far as she could go. Her mouth was wet and perfect but he needed more. So much more. He needed all of her.

"Layla," he groaned, his body bowstring tight with anticipation.

She kept sweetly teasing him, her tongue swirling around the sensitive head. He held off as long as he could, groaning again as he threaded his fingers through her thick, dark hair. The mass of it fell around his hips in waves as she continued her sweet, sweet torture.

I'm too close. And he wasn't coming in her mouth this time. No, he wanted to be inside her.

Beyond words at this point, he tightened his grip in her hair.

She looked up at him, her expression pure, wicked sensuality. To his surprise she didn't tease him. Instead, she shimmied up his body, straddling him before she wrapped her fingers around his erection. Then she slid on to him.

And at that moment he truly did forget to breathe— to think—as she sank all the way down on him.

As she settled, she sucked in a sharp breath, staring down at him with heavy-lidded eyes. "So big," she gasped out.

And again, he felt like a fucking god.

Though he wanted her to ride him, he needed to take control. This time at least. He was on a tightrope and needed to take the edge off.

Moving swiftly, but not disengaging from her, he shifted their bodies so he was on top of her. He didn't start thrusting though. Not yet. He wanted her to adjust to him and he desperately wanted her to come again. The other night he'd made sure she had more than once and he would do the same now. She was his to take care of for as long as they had together.

He was going to imprint himself on her so she never forgot him. Sliding his fingers through her hair, he cupped the back of her head and kissed her again, tasting the woman who could never fully be his.

When she started rolling her hips upward, silent little demands for more, he finally began thrusting, in and out. Over and over.

He was addicted to her. Couldn't get enough of her.

He felt possessed as she wrapped her arms around his back, digging her fingers into his ass, urging him on.

"Yes, more," she demanded.

It was that fiery little tone, her hot demands, that almost pushed him over the edge. Almost.

But he reached between their bodies and began strumming her clit. Apparently she was just as close as he was because she surged into climax with very little teasing, her inner walls tightening around his cock as he found his own release.

They lost themselves in each other completely, until he lost track of time, until the only thing that existed was her and him. The house was secure, as was the perimeter he'd set up, so he was free to enjoy every second with his Layla.

His.

And he was hers because she had completely claimed him. She owned a part of him he'd thought was long dead.

Now that it had woken up, it was going to slice him up to let her go.

* * *

Layla stepped out from under the stream of the shower jets as she heard the bathroom door opening, anticipation humming through her. A second later the shower door opened and Xavier stared at her, with hunger and a thousand other emotions, for a long moment. She stood there unabashedly as he drank her in. She loved the way he looked at her—the way she felt when he did.

His blatant desire for her made her feel powerful in front of this strong man who'd completely claimed her heart. She was ignoring the fact that soon her heart would be broken when he walked away. She'd told him she was fine with right now—which was a mix of truth and lies. She wasn't fine, but she'd take the time she could have with him. He was worth it.

"Are you planning on joining me?" she murmured. After they'd had sex in front of the fireplace, then again upstairs, he'd made them breakfast. And then gone down on her again.

He was insatiable. And so was she.

"I want to," he rasped out, regret in his expression. "But Gage just made contact. They have a lead on the Murphy brothers."

His words were like cold water slapping against her face. The information should make her happy—and it did. But she knew this was the beginning of the end for her and Xavier. "Are they going after them?"

"It sounds as if they want to bring the brothers out in the open."

"How?"

"Bait them," he said, his gaze flicking down to her breasts.

Sighing, she reached over and turned the water off. He automatically handed her a towel and a thick, cotton robe. "How, exactly?" she asked.

"I'm not sure of the details, but you and I are headed back to Redemption Harbor as soon as you can pack. I'm going to be part of the takedown team so they're waiting for us." There was more than a hint of anger in his voice.

Which she understood. These men had targeted her to hurt him. And after she'd read the files Xavier had on them, she had no pity for them or their dead brother. Growing up in the foster system, she'd seen her share of monsters and assholes. "Do we have time for…anything else before we leave?" she asked as she tightened the sash around her waist. She didn't come out and say *sex*, but it should be pretty clear what she meant. Even though she wanted these men caught, she was definitely stalling. As soon as they made it to Redemption Harbor it would be back to reality.

Then…Xavier would walk out of her life for good.

His green eyes were heavy-lidded as he pulled her into his arms, but he simply kissed her forehead. Sighing, he ran a hand over her wet hair. "I want to stay here with you, but we need to get back as soon as possible."

She buried her face against his chest and held on to him tight. The countdown was officially on because she had no doubt that between him and the Redemption Harbor crew's skills, the Murphy brothers would be captured very soon.

Then everything would change. Just the thought of a life without Xavier made her chest hurt. He was determined to cut ties with her once this was all over and she wasn't going to beg him to stay. If he stayed, he had to do it of his own accord. "I hate all of this," she said quietly. Okay, so she might not beg, but she was going to be honest about how this made her feel.

"I do too," he said, resting his chin on top of her head.

But he didn't say he'd changed his mind, that he'd been a fool to think he could walk away from her. Nope, he didn't say anything at all.

And that was answer enough for her. It hurt. To be fair, he'd been honest with her about what he could give her. She wasn't surprised but...her heart still ached.

CHAPTER SEVENTEEN

—Friends and wine...the older, the better.—

"What's wrong?" Layla asked as Xavier turned off the engine in front of the Redemption Harbor Consulting warehouse.

What's wrong? He didn't want to get out. After hours of driving with her to Redemption Harbor, he didn't want to be separated from her. But unfortunately it was back to the real world.

And after this was over, he would have to walk away from her. He didn't see any other way if he ultimately wanted her to be happy. Safe. "I just don't want to go in there," he said, referring to the warehouse where the Redemption Harbor crew worked. He was surprised they'd even told him where it was located. It wasn't the building listed on their official tax or real estate papers, but the actual building where the team met. This invite meant they trusted him to an impressive degree. He wasn't sure what to do with that knowledge. "I don't want to go in there," he said simply. "I do, but I don't."

"I know, but you want to be part of this takedown," Layla said, her voice quiet, her expression somber.

He wanted to deny it, to leave right now with her, but it was true. Xavier had no doubt that this group could take down the Murphy brothers without his assistance, but it was his fault these guys were after Layla, and there was no way he would sit back and let anyone else take charge of this op. It wasn't like he needed to give orders or be a fucking team leader, but he *would* be part of the crew to bring down the Murphy brothers. He needed to see with his own eyes that they were stopped.

He reached across the center console and slid his fingers through her soft, smaller ones. "The last twenty-four hours with you have been incredible." He wished he could convey more of what the last day had meant to him. He was completely in love with her and wasn't sure if he should tell her. He didn't know if it would make things better or worse—for both of them. And walking away from her was already going to be the hardest thing he'd ever done.

"I know," she whispered, leaning over to brush her soft lips against his.

It took all of his self-control to not take her right there in the front seat of the SUV. *Hell.* Clearing his throat, he pulled back. "Let's head in there." Then he rounded the vehicle and took her hand in his as she stepped out of the front seat.

She didn't need his help, but he simply wanted to touch her for as long as he could. As they approached the nondescript side door, it swung open. Nova rushed out, her dark hair in a messy bun, her expression relieved as she pulled Layla into a big hug.

Xavier still didn't drop her hand. He couldn't force himself to let Layla go even as she hugged her best friend. He needed to be touching her.

Nova's eyes widened slightly as she stepped back and saw that they were holding hands, but she simply smiled at him and gave him an awkward shoulder pat. "Let's get you guys inside. Gage has narrowed down where he thinks these assholes are and it sounds as if they've come up with a good plan to bring them out into the open. They're being more careful than we like, so we've got to draw them to us."

Minutes later he found himself in a plush conference room with state-of-the-art technology, expensive, modern furniture and odd paintings of dancing sea creatures and pets dressed in human clothing on one of the walls. On the longest wall was a sea of computer screens.

Most of those were dark, but the cluster in the middle had various information onscreen regarding intel Xavier had given Gage—including some of his past kills and info on the Murphy brothers. It was weird to see aspects of his life on view like that but he ignored it as he sat down at one end with Layla. He wanted to pull her into his lap and wrap his arms around her but wasn't sure how she would react to that in front of her friends, so instead he sat directly next to her and continued holding her hand. He shifted back in surprise when a little black-and-white dog came up to him, smelled his ankle, then turned around, completely disinterested.

"C-4 only likes you if you give him treats," Skye said, scooping up the tiny dog who licked her cheek in complete adoration.

"Did she just say C-4?" he asked Layla quietly.

Layla snorted. "Yep. She named her dog C-4."

Okay, then.

"All right, the plan is simple," Colt said, standing at one end of the long table. "We have a general location of the Murphy brothers but we can't pinpoint them to an exact address."

Gage muttered a curse about that, but Colt just side-eyed him before continuing.

"So instead of sitting around and waiting, we're going to bring them to us using Layla's cell phone. She's going to make a scripted phone call to Nova, and we're hoping they're tracking her enough to pinpoint where she is. We've got a whole script that should make it clear you think you're safe for now. From there, we'll wait for them to come out in the open."

"Layla isn't going to be bait," Xavier snapped, horrified at the very idea. He'd been under the impression that they had a different type of plan laid out when Gage had contacted him.

Layla gently squeezed his hand. "Xavier—"

"Of course she's not," Skye said. "I'm going to be the one waiting for these morons. You're obviously going to be there as well. The rest of the crew will be working as backup and some will be in the house we'll be holed up in—but only two heat signatures will be visible from the outside. I've done this type of bait and switch thing before. Multiple times. Hell, we all have," she said, gesturing to the others at the table. "The way we're setting this thing up, these fools won't get close enough to see my actual face. We just need to get them to where we want them. Then..." She lifted a shoulder, not needing to say more.

Then, the Murphy brothers died. At least that was Xavier's plan. He didn't care what the others wanted, though he guessed they could want to simply capture the brothers.

"Okay." Xavier settled back in his chair, listening as they laid out the rest of the plan.

As long as Layla was safe, that was all he cared about. Keeping her alive so she could go on living.

Even though it had to be without him.

* * *

"I hate that Skye is going to be bait," Layla said to Nova, not bothering to hide her worry since it was just the two of them in the break room. The others were going over the "operation" plans and Layla would be staying in this warehouse for the time being. They weren't sure how long it would take to bring the Murphy brothers out into the open, so until then she was staying put.

Brooks had offered to let her stay on his sprawling ranch—which she'd been to before—but for now she'd decided to stay here. She didn't want to bring any danger to his family there, even though he'd assured her it was completely safe. Maybe if this went on for a while she'd relocate to the Alexander Ranch but the warehouse worked fine. Considering Xavier wasn't going anywhere, she was making this her home base too since she didn't want to be far from him.

"She's done this type of thing before, trust me," Nova said. "She's a fucking badass. If anything, I feel bad for those guys."

Layla smiled. "True enough. I just hate this feeling of helplessness. I feel so useless." And if she was being honest, a little worthless. But she knew that was the little voice in her head talking. The one that sounded like her dead bitch of a mother.

"So what's up with you and Xavier?" Nova asked pointedly as she grabbed a little canister of chocolates off the countertop. She screwed off the top and held the canister out to Layla.

Grabbing a handful of Reese's, she said, "I don't know what to say, honestly. I had the best sex of my life with him. More than once. But he thinks that once this is over, he needs to leave my life for good. And I didn't ask him for anything long-term because I'm not going to beg, so it's not like he's being a jerk. I wanted... I just wanted to be with him while I could," she said, unable to keep the sadness out of her voice. Because it sucked. There was no way around it. Right now simply sucked and her heart hurt with the knowledge that as soon as this was done, Xavier would be out of her life forever. She would never talk to him again, never see him. Because he didn't seem like the kind of man who did things halfway. He would split, and she'd have a broken heart. She'd lose the only man she'd ever loved.

"Oh, honey." Nova reached out and pulled her into a tight hug. "I swear I'll get you wine as soon as I can. I think Skye's got a hidden stash in her office. Wine and chocolate might not fix things, but they'll help," she said against the top of Layla's head, her voice muffled.

Layla hugged her best friend back and held her tears at bay. Barely.

Because she knew that if she let them out now, she might not stop. And she wasn't going to cry when the others were literally walking into danger as soon as the Murphy brothers showed themselves. So she would bury all her emotions deep down and deal with things as well as she could. She'd compartmentalize like she always had. "I want Pinot Grigio," she muttered, making Nova's body shake with laughter.

"I'll get you whatever you want," her best friend said.

CHAPTER EIGHTEEN

—Family is everything.—

Xavier paced inside the split-level home they were holed up in. On a lake in Redemption Harbor, the home was far enough away from its neighbors that the team had decided it was the perfect place to lure the Murphy brothers to.

Gage had set things up so that it looked as if Xavier had rented the house under an alias and was staying here with Layla. Then Gage had worked his magic and right now it appeared as if there were only two heat signatures in the house. That was some next-gen shit and Xavier could admit he was impressed.

Still, he felt like a caged tiger, stuck in this house and far from Layla when danger was coming. It was a double-edged sword. He didn't want her anywhere near him, but at the same time he wanted to be able to protect her, to see with his own eyes that she was safe. They'd FaceTimed more than once but it wasn't the same as seeing her in person, holding her. Kissing her. Especially since when this was over, he'd lose her.

"Why don't you hit the treadmill in the gym?" Skye said as she strode into the living room. Wearing workout gear, her hair pulled back in a tight braid, it looked as if she'd just come from there. Her fists were also wrapped up as if she'd been pounding on a punching bag. "It's free right now."

He rolled his shoulders once. "I've already worked out twice today."

"All right. I can kick your ass in poker if you're feeling up to it."

He found himself unexpectedly laughing at her dry tone. "I don't know about that. I'm pretty good."

She lifted an eyebrow. "Put your money where your mouth is."

Her husband strode in then and looked between the two of them. "I hope you have deep pockets," he muttered. "She's a savage when it comes to cards."

"I could play a few hands," Xavier said, despite the warning. He needed the distraction.

Half turning toward the hallway, Colt shouted, "Savage, get your ass down here."

Minutes later the four of them sat around the table playing poker. "This reminds me of the Corps," Xavier said absently.

Savage smiled and folded. "Yeah no kidding, though we played for a lot less then."

"You were in the Marines too?"

"Yeah. Force Recon."

He nodded once. "I served with Axel, something you probably already know."

"We know a lot about you," Skye said. "So are you sticking around after we take out the assholes?" she asked pointedly.

"Skye." Colt shook his head. "We are not having this conversation."

She lifted a shoulder. "Why not? I want to know." She turned to look at Xavier, pinning him with a hard stare. "Are you staying or leaving? It's an easy answer."

He didn't shy away from it. "It's probably better if I leave."

"That's not exactly an answer."

"If I stay, I'll just put Layla in danger again."

"That's a possibility. But her being friends with us puts her in danger too. And her ex-fiancé put her in danger as well. There aren't any fucking guarantees in this world. But you do what you gotta do. If you stay, we want to talk to you about working with us. Of course that's only if you don't fuck up this operation." Grinning, she laid down a royal flush. "And I win. Again. Suckers!" Laughing like a lunatic, she gathered all the bills on the table and started making little piles. "I'm going to call this my Colt pile and roll around in it later."

Colt snorted, giving his wife a sideways glance.

As he digested her words, Xavier tossed his cards onto the table and looked at the other two men. "You guys want to...hire me?"

They both nodded.

"We would have approached you in a different manner than Skye," Savage said, rolling his eyes. "But yes. If you decide to stay in Redemption Harbor, we'd like to recruit you. We've already gone over your file and it's impressive."

Of course they'd gone over his file. Probably with a fine-tooth comb. The thought of working with them was intriguing, but he mentally shook himself. He didn't *want* to leave. That much he knew. But he also didn't want Layla in danger because of him. There wasn't a good choice for either of them.

"You've been doing what you've been doing for quite a while," Colt said. "And this is the first time you've ever been outright targeted, right?"

"Yes." He was very careful about covering his tracks. He had family to think about. And now Layla.

"So it stands to reason that someone spent a whole lot of money hunting you down. If you continue doing what you do, you'll probably be targeted again. But if you quit, the chances of someone coming after you again are pretty slim. Not to mention Gage is already building up an extra layer, to insulate you from this happening again."

"He is?" That surprised him.

Colt nodded once, then slid one card over to Skye, their dealer. "Yep. He's doing it for free. So whether you work with us or not, we've still got your back."

Hell. That had just made his decision a lot harder. And it wasn't easy to begin with. Because every time he FaceTimed with Layla and saw her, he couldn't imagine walking away from her. All right, every time he even *thought* about her—which was approximately every two-point-two seconds, he couldn't imagine walking away from her. Now to have a job offer like this, one he fig-ured he could probably do fairly well, considering what he knew about this crew? One that would give him roots and a job that shouldn't put Layla in danger? How the hell was he going to walk away from her after this?

* * *

Two days later

"I recognize that look," Savage said to Xavier as they waited in one of the rooms, watching a couple video screens of their incoming targets.

Gage had just informed them that the Murphy brothers were on the property and doing recon of the house. Soon this thing should be over, one way or another.

Xavier wasn't sure what kind of next-generation technology the crew was using, but he'd seen with his own eyes that only two heat signatures were available from the outside, not four. And the Murphy brothers would definitely cover their asses in that regard.

Now, after two days of waiting, they'd finally showed up. They'd taken the bait. Supposedly.

"What look?" he asked.

"The one that says you're ready to put a bullet in both of their heads." Savage's tone was dry.

Xavier had gotten to know the guy a little over the last couple days and he genuinely liked him. Hell, he liked everyone who was part of this crew. They lived their lives the way they wanted, mostly in shades of gray, and he could relate to that. Because the world was never black and white, no matter how much people wanted it to be. At least not in his experience.

"Yeah, I want to kill them both. And I think it's stupid that we're not going to." More than stupid. He wanted these two threats eliminated for good.

"We kill if we have to. We need to find out how these guys found you and who else knows about you and Layla. They've got multiple warrants out for their arrest so once we're done with them, we'll gift them to the FBI or DEA. Whoever picks them up first."

Xavier simply grunted. "Fine. But I'm using lethal force if I don't have a choice." He'd never been trigger-happy before. He was always in control, only taking out the necessary targets, but these men had wanted to hurt Layla. Knowing how vile they were, they would have done more than simply kidnap her and use her against him. They would've hurt her badly. For that alone he wanted to rip their throats out, and it was hard to hide that kind of rage.

Savage simply grunted before turning back to the screens set up in the bedroom.

Xavier watched with him.

Two figures were on opposite sides of the property, clearly visible on the hidden video cameras Gage had put everywhere. Even though the men were separated, the two of them moved like a cohesive unit, circling the house like predators. Too bad for them they were prey.

Xavier checked both his weapons just for good measure and waited.

Then waited some more.

"How are you guys doing in the kitchen?" Xavier murmured to Skye and Colt over the comm line.

"Good," Colt said just as Skye said, "Ready to kick some ass."

He grinned to himself despite the entire situation. Something told him that if he took a job with this crew he would never be bored. And he couldn't believe he was even contemplating taking a job with them. He should be preparing to leave Layla.

But he shoved those thoughts away. He couldn't afford to give her any of his headspace. He needed to be totally focused on this job, focusing on bringing these guys down. Eliminating the threat to her so she could sleep easy at night.

So she would be safe.

One of the figures turned away from the house but the other kept going toward the east side of it. Xavier frowned, wondering what the guy was doing. But then he saw the other one had circled back and was following after his brother. They weren't going to enter from different points, but the same one. Probably because they saw the two heat signatures in the kitchen. They would either go in weapons blazing using a shock and awe tactic or try to sneak in through another point and attempt to ambush.

When the two figures continued past the kitchen door, he watched the monitor as they moved to one of the back bedrooms. The lights weren't on in that particular room so maybe that was why they'd chosen it as a point of entry.

At the window, the men paused, surveying the seams. Then one of them gently nudged the other. Using hand gestures, they both slowly backed away from the window.

Shit.

Xavier's instinct told him that the men were bailing. Their body language screamed that they had been spooked. Next to him, Savage straightened as well as he muttered a curse under his breath.

"Gage, what's your status?" Skye asked into the ear comm.

The rest of the Redemption Harbor crew were nearby waiting as backup, but they hadn't gotten too close to the house. Their job had been to run extra recon, watching in case more backup arrived for the Murphy brothers.

"Still in place. Nothing has changed on my end. No new tangos."

The others all murmured the affirmative as well. No backup for the brothers was a good thing.

"It looks like they're headed north on foot toward the water," Xavier said even though Savage could see the same as well, as the screen shifted to a new image, showing the men leaving.

Gage had set up cameras all around the property so they had eyes everywhere.

"Something spooked them," Skye said. "Maybe they saw one of our cameras."

"Or maybe it was simply their sixth sense," Xavier said, already moving into action. He withdrew one of his weapons, heading for the back of the house. Those cameras were hidden damn well. Even if you knew where they were, it was almost impossible to see them. No, if he had to guess, the Murphy brothers were listening to their well-honed instincts telling them danger was near. Too bad it wasn't going to be enough.

"What are you doing?" Savage asked, following after him.

"What the hell does it look like? I'm going after them. I don't work for you guys. And this is my decision. I'm not letting them get away."

"He's right," Colt said over the comm. "We've gotta tail them."

Xavier headed out the back door, ready for battle, and to do this with or without the team. "What's their location?"

"Headed north toward the lake," Gage said. "Looks as if they'll try to cut through a neighbor's property east after that, but I'm going to lose visual of them soon."

Adrenaline punched through Xavier as he raced across the backyard, his legs eating up the distance across it. There was barely any illumination as clouds covered the nearly full moon. Using that to his advantage he sprinted, glad for his daily workouts.

"Right behind you," Savage murmured, his voice clear through Xavier's earpiece.

"We're circling up through the front yard and will head parallel to you guys." Skye's words were clipped. "Stay in contact."

"I've lost visual of both of you," Gage said.

Xavier slowed then as he reached a long line of eight-foot-high hedges, spaced about a foot apart. Savage did the same, then motioned that he'd head right, so Xavier went left. They'd done enough recon of the immediate area that they knew the neighbors here were out of town—which was part of the reason they'd chosen this locale—and since each home was on about two acres there was a whole lot of space between the lake area and the homes.

Moving swiftly, he ducked through the hedges, quickly scanning for signs of movement as the clouds shifted and the moonlight illuminated everything with spotlight clarity. The Olympic- sized pool to his right glistened but was still. The lake was placid as well. Where the hell were they— *There.*

A human shadow peeled off an oak tree about thirty feet from the shoreline. Then another one.

Xavier took off.

Pfft, pfft.

Dirt flew up next to his feet as someone shot at him using a suppressor.

So much for no lethal force.

Still running, Xavier lifted his weapon, aimed and fired at one of the shadows.

"Aghh," someone cried out in agony as the shadow slumped to the earth.

"Hit one of them," he murmured.

"I'm at your five o'clock and moving in. Don't shoot me," Savage said, just as quietly.

"You see the other one?" he asked, closing in on the fallen man.

"He kept going into the cluster of trees but it could be a trap."

Yeah, Xavier had thought of that too. He was ninety-nine percent sure his aim was true, but he was going to be careful.

Pfft, pfft. The familiar sound of bullets leaving a silenced weapon filled the air.

Pain sliced down Xavier's upper arm as he moved in on the nearest target.

He fired back into the darkness of the trees just as Savage said, "I'm going after him."

With the moonlight highlighting everything it was damn near impossible to gain cover. Weapon still in hand, white-hot pain ripping through his arm, he aimed at the fallen man and reached out to test his pulse.

The man rolled over, brandishing his pistol.

Xavier kicked out, slamming into the guy's arm. The weapon went flying but the man shifted his entire body, sweeping Xavier's legs out from under him.

Still holding his weapon, he fell backward, kicking out as he did. *Fucking hell.* He bit back a cry of pain.

"Umph." The man grunted as Xavier made contact with something.

Even as Xavier fell again, he started to roll, ready to shoot when the man dove, tackling him.

Xavier's pistol fell from his hand as a fist smashed into his spine.

Pain exploded in his back but he slammed his elbow backward, connecting with bone.

"Fuck," the man cried out.

Xavier turned fully, took a punch across the jaw. With a left hook from his uninjured arm, he took the guy off guard and slammed his fist into the man's nose with a crunch. Blood spurted everywhere as the guy's head jerked back.

Xavier reached out, grabbed his pistol from the grass. As he turned back, the man had a knife raised, ready to slam it into his chest.

He fired. Two shots to the chest.

Eyes wide, the man froze in place, as if suspended by a string. Just as suddenly, someone cut the strings and his body slumped forward.

Moving out of the way, Xavier dodged getting covered in the guy's blood. At a slight shuffling sound, he was on his feet, weapon up. His adrenaline was high, muting most of his pain.

"Just us," Skye said as she approached, her expression grim in the moonlight. "You shot?"

"Wh..." He glanced at his upper arm and found it covered in blood. "Nicked, I think. Barely broke the skin." Still fucking hurt though.

"Other one's down." Savage's voice came over the comm line crystal clear.

"Damn it," Skye muttered.

Xavier knew he should probably show some concern that the men were dead but he didn't care. He was *glad* the threat to Layla was over. These two assholes were only known for working with Brant Clark and Calvin Long—and he'd made sure those fuckers were dead. "How are we going to do this?" Meaning, how would they dispose of the bodies? He knew how he usually worked, but this whole team thing was new to him.

"We've got a vehicle on standby for transport," was all she said.

All right, then. He wasn't part of their crew and they didn't want to tell him how they got rid of bodies. Fair enough. "Gage, can you tell Layla she's likely safe?" Maybe not completely but she was safe of this threat and she deserved to know immediately. Xavier didn't have his phone on him—they were all dark for this for the most part—and Gage would be able to tell her quickest. And Xavier didn't want one more second to pass than necessary where Layla feared for her life.

"Already done."

Good. Though he was going to insist she stay in hiding for a little while. At least until they fully ran the records of the Murphy brothers to see if they were hiding any other secrets.

CHAPTER NINETEEN

—Everyone has baggage. Find someone who loves
you enough to help you unpack.—

L ayla jumped slightly, pushing one of the decorative
couch cushions off her as her phone buzzed against
the glass and steel side table next to her. The Redemption Harbor crew had deemed a new complex owned by
one of Brooks's companies the perfect safe house because
of the security. So she'd been holed up here the last four-
teen hours, more or less feeling like a nomad.

A few hours ago she'd gotten the call that the team
had found and "dispatched" the Murphy brothers—and it
hadn't been Xavier on the line. She'd demanded to know
whether he was okay, and since then she hadn't been able
to go back to sleep. And pretty much no one had the
number to her burner phone so it had to be one of them.

"It's me." Xavier sounded exhausted. "I'm coming in
and didn't want to scare you."

"Okay." Relief punched through her as she hung up
and hurried out of the spacious living room. She was
barely aware of moving as she made it to the foyer just
as he stepped inside, locking the door behind him. She
was desperate to see him at this point, even if she knew
this was the beginning of the end for them. He was okay
and that was what mattered.

"I wanted to make sure I wasn't followed before heading over here, or I'd have been here a lot earlier."

"It's fine," she said, rushing toward him. She pulled him into a big hug but froze when he slightly winced. "What?" she asked, worried. Dammit, something *had* happened to him and no one had told her.

"It's nothing. Just...I kind of got nicked."

"Nicked?"

"With a bullet."

"Oh my God!" How was he being all casual? And why wasn't he at a doctor's? "Xavier—"

"It's fine, I swear." His smile was wry as he pulled her into another hug, this one a lot gentler. "It didn't break any skin. Not really. I don't even need stitches. It's like a cat scratched me. I literally just have a small wrap on my upper arm."

Even though his explanation soothed her—for the moment, because she was going to insist on seeing his bandaged arm—she buried her face against his chest and was careful not to jostle him too much. "So what happens now? Am I still in danger?" She'd talked to Nova a little bit but she still had a lot of questions. So. Many. Questions.

"Let's talk in the kitchen. Does this place have any coffee?"

"Yes and I have a fresh pot on. I haven't been able to sleep since I got Gage's call earlier."

He slid an arm around her shoulders, pulling her close, and she allowed herself a little hope that maybe he'd changed his mind about the future. About them. About everything.

"Sit." She pointed at one of the barstools along the edge of the kitchen bar. "I don't want you doing anything right now." She started getting him coffee and breakfast that consisted of fruit and yogurt because she was sure he probably hadn't eaten. The rest of the team had been holed up at some sort of safe house, and if she had to guess, they'd probably all eaten like teenage boys.

"We can't know for sure that the threat to you is gone, but historically speaking, anyone associated with the brothers is already dead. Gage is going to be tearing apart their lives to see if anyone else was involved with this, but if not, you'll be free to return to life as normal."

"Will my life include you?" she asked boldly as she set the plate of fruit in front of him.

He choked on his coffee for a moment as he set the mug down. "You're just getting right to it, aren't you?"

"I am. I know what we agreed on and I just want to know if you've changed your mind." Because she wanted him in her life and in her bed. For always.

"I haven't," he said, making her heart drop like a rock. "I want to. I want to stay more than anything but I won't put you in danger like that." His expression was stoic as he spoke, his body completely rigid.

"So you're just going to keep doing what you do?"

"I didn't say that."

Yeah well, he didn't not say it. "So are you quitting?"

"I'm contemplating it."

A spark of hope kindled inside her. "So even if you quit, you wouldn't stay?" She wrapped her arms around herself as she stared at him across the little marble-topped bar. How could he not stay? Did he not feel the same as she did?

"Not right now. I think you need time to decide whether you really want to be with me or not anyway."

She snorted at that, angry and insulted. "That's bull-shit and you know it. You know what I want. I want a future with you. And if you didn't know, I'm laying it out very clearly for you right now. So if you leave, it's on you. It's your choice. I'm willing to deal with any potential threats if you stay and quit your current profession. I think you're worth it." She wasn't saying the actual words *I love you* but her statement was pretty damn clear. "I think *we're* worth it."

He left his plate in front of him, mostly untouched, his expression tormented. "Layla... Fuck."

"Unless you say that you're going to stay, don't say anything." She rounded the island and shifted so she was in between his legs. Gently she placed her hands on his shoulders.

"I can't stay," he whispered. "I'm no good for you."

She fought the tears, the pain that slid through her rib cage as she thought of a life without him. But instead of crying, she leaned forward, brushing her lips over his.

Immediately he deepened the kiss, taking over and apparently not caring about his arm as he stood and pulled her up so that she had to wrap her legs around his waist.

One more time. That was all she was going to allow herself with him.

One day. Right now. Then she had to cut all ties if she was going to stay sane. Because if he wasn't quitting his job, if she wasn't enough reason for him to stay here, she couldn't let this drag on any longer than that. It would rip her heart out otherwise.

But she also couldn't walk away from him right now, couldn't say no to his kisses, his caresses.

And when he lifted her up and carried her to the bedroom, she took all he had to offer, took his tenderness as he made love to her, kissing her as if he would die without his mouth on hers.

The pleasure he gave her was bittersweet, mixed in with the knowledge that he'd be leaving soon, that this was all the time they had together.

Once they were both spent, she held on to him, burying her face against his chest, inhaling his masculine scent and memorizing it.

"I got you something," Xavier murmured against the top of her hair, their naked bodies intertwined against the soft, tangled sheets.

She didn't trust her voice enough to work, and when he produced a necklace from his discarded pants pocket, tears stung her eyes. She'd sworn she wouldn't cry, but she couldn't hold anything back now.

"Don't cry," he murmured, his own voice thick as he clasped it around her neck. "It'll get easier."

So why didn't he sound like he believed his own words? It wasn't going to get easier. It was going to be harder once he left and took part of her heart with him.

So she kissed him again, hard this time, determined to banish some of her tears for now as she lost herself in his arms one more time.

Just once more. That was all her heart could take.

CHAPTER TWENTY

—Wine and cupcakes are great for book club. And
pity parties.—

Two weeks later

"Ah, hey guys...what's going on?" Layla asked as a sudden troop of her friends—eight of them—marched into the oversized, luxurious kitchen at the Alexander Ranch. She'd been lying low here the last two weeks even though the crew was almost positive the threat to her was gone.

She felt like a coward, hiding out from the rest of the world. She could have gone back to her house—well, Nova's house—a few days ago, but the thought of doing so was depressing. Especially since she had a lot of memories with Xavier there. Hanging out in a giant mansion on a thousand-plus-acre spread of land also wasn't the worst thing in the world. They had an actual movie room here that was insane.

"We've got cupcakes and other treats for you." Nova set a giant bakery box on the center island.

"And trust me," Mary Grace said, setting down another box, "this idea is a heck of a lot better than what Skye wanted to do."

205

"I still say my idea is the best. Trust *me*," she said, looking at Layla as she grabbed a cannoli out of one of the boxes. "An hour on the shooting range would help expel a whole lot of your rage. But cupcakes are okay, I guess."

She laughed lightly. Skye had forced her to go to the shooting range more than once. Layla might not care for guns in the general sense, but she liked knowing how to use one at least. If she could use it, it was less likely to be turned on her. And she was less likely to be a victim ever again. "I'm really happy to see all of you, but I still don't understand why you guys are here."

Filling the kitchen were Skye, Nova, Mary Grace, Olivia, Darcy, Martina, Hadley and even Lucy, who she was still getting to know.

"Because we're friends," Olivia said. "And you are clearly in need of some pastry therapy."

"It's only nine o'clock in the morning." Still, she peeked into one of the boxes, her mouth watering at the sight of all the sugary confection. Cupcakes for breakfast sounded like a fine idea. She grabbed one with multicolored rainbow frosting on top. "Where's Valencia?" she asked.

"Hanging with Savage and some of the guys," Olivia said, snagging a cupcake for herself. "And probably getting super spoiled."

"Those men are ridiculous," Mary Grace said. "And my own husband is the worst."

Valencia was Olivia's seven-year-old daughter and Savage was her adopted dad. She was one of the sweetest little kids Layla had ever met. She was the kind of kid Layla would love to have in a classroom. Kind to others and eager to learn. She was also the reason Layla was now taking ASL classes.

"I say we plan a spa day next week as well," Martina, the fiancée of billionaire Douglas Alexander said, perching on the edge of one of the barstools at the island. She didn't live in the main house where Layla was staying, but out with Douglas on a home a couple miles away on the huge spread of property. She'd been over the last couple weeks and hadn't even bothered to hide the fact that she was checking in on Layla.

"I'm actually down with that," Layla said. "And I'm not over here feeling sorry for myself." As everyone looked at her with disbelieving gazes, she tossed up her hands. "Fine. Maybe I'm having a little bit of a pity party but I think that's okay. The man I...love is gone. He made the decision to walk out of my life and there's nothing I can do. It sucks and I don't feel like pretending I'm okay with it. Which is why I've been hiding out here bingeing different TV shows."

"It's good to admit that it sucks," Mary Grace said quietly.

"Did you tell him you love him?" Nova asked after a long pause.

She shook her head. Normally she would have told Nova by now but Layla had retreated into herself since Xavier had left. She hadn't wanted to talk to anyone about anything. "What would be the point? I was trying to hold on to some of my pride."

Darcy nodded sympathetically. "I get it. I really, really do." She lifted out a pink and white petit four with immaculately manicured fingers. "Relationships are hard. And men are kind of thick sometimes."

There were lots of snorts and murmurs of agreement, which made Layla feel a whole lot better. After losing Xavier, she felt like she was missing part of herself. She was going to let herself grieve over the loss of what could have been.

"Look, even though I'm totally feeling sorry for myself, I really am okay. Starting Monday, I have a plan to get things back on track." Again. "I've sent out résumés for permanent teaching positions instead of just accepting substitute jobs. And I'm still looking for a new place to live. I'm putting down roots here."

"You know you can stay at my house as long as you want," Nova said.

"I do know that. But I need something that's just mine. I'm kind of looking for a fixer-upper. Something I can work on in my spare time and keep myself busy. Not falling down around my ears type of fixer-upper, but something that needs TLC."

"Well Axel loves fixing stuff up," Hadley said. "So if you do get a fixer-upper, let us know. And when I say us, I mean him. He will *gladly* help with anything."

Layla grinned at her friend, positive Axel would do anything his wife asked of him with a smile on his face.

Two hours later, the women had slowly started drifting out, so it was just Layla, Nova and Skye.

"The offer for an hour at the gun range still stands. You're out of practice anyway." Skye pulled her into a hug that was almost normal for her. Since Layla had gotten to know Skye, the woman's hugs had become less and less awkward, as if she was getting used to displays of affection.

"That works for me. And you only owe me one pedicure day instead of two."

Skye rolled her eyes. "Fine."

"Don't act like you didn't like it last time."

"Colt certainly liked that ridiculous, sparkly pedicure you made me get. He sucked on my—" Skye's eyes widened as if she realized what she'd been about to say.

Layla burst out laughing. "Oh my God, I'm going to want more details later."

Skye simply pressed her pointer finger and thumb together and ran them over her mouth, miming that she was zipping her lips up.

"Yeah, we'll see. Pervert."

"I am a *huge* pervert. Never denied that." Skye grinned as she grabbed one of the leftover boxes of treats before heading out of the kitchen.

"Feeling better?" Only Nova remained now, sipping on a cup of tea.

"You know, I really am. Being here the past couple weeks has probably only added to my depression, but knowing I've got an amazing support system has brought me back to reality. Losing Xavier hurts so much worse than I imagined but...I'll rebound." Eventually.

She hoped. *Ugh.* If she kept telling herself that, maybe it would be true. But it wouldn't be today.

At a little dinging sound, she glanced at her cell phone and pulled open the message when she saw that it was from her Realtor.

Found the perfect home for you. On one acre. Three bed, two bath, lots of privacy. Everything upgraded. In your price range and the area you wanted. Not listed yet so they're open to offers. See attached pictures.

Her eyes widened when she looked at the images. A cute little ranch home under her budget. With the exception of the upgrades—she really had been looking forward to some reno projects—that sounded like something she wanted to see. "Hang on, Nova. Gotta text my Realtor back." She quickly typed in, *When can I see it?*

ASAP. I'm showing a few homes today but I can see you in the next hour or so.

Sounds good. Just tell me what time and I'll be there.

"What did she say?" Nova asked as Layla set her phone down.

"My Realtor found a place she thinks I might like so I'm going to see it today."

"Want company?"

"Nah. Spend the rest of the day with your man. Thank you for setting this whole thing up though." Because Layla had no doubt that it was her best friend who'd asked everyone to come over here today.

"What are friends for? Having your heart broken sucks."

"Yeah it does. So did Gage ever find out any more on the Murphy brothers? If they'd been working with anyone else?" Layla figured they'd have told her any discoveries, but she still wanted to ask.

"He finally found the place the brothers had been holed up at. I know Gage is combing over their tablets and laptop right now but most of that is just automated stuff. He's also been listening for any chatter about Xavier or you and it's been silent. So it's not as if there's a contract out on either of you...which was our worry."

The thought of someone having a contract out on her was beyond surreal. "Good. Tell him I really appreciate it. Also...I hate to even ask about him, but any news about Xavier?"

Nova paused, biting her bottom lip.

"What?"

"I don't know if I should tell you."

Dread filled Layla as she imagined her best friend telling her the worst, that Xavier had already moved on and found someone new. That everything he'd told her had been a lie. That it hadn't been hard at all for him to walk away and she was a pathetic fool. "What?" she demanded.

"Well...he's still in Redemption Harbor. At least that's what Gage said. And I don't know why," Nova tacked on quickly.

"He is?" she asked more out of shock because there was no way Nova would lie to her.

Nova nodded. "Yep."

Layla digested that information as best she could. "I don't even know what to do with that."

On instinct she reached out to touch the necklace he'd given her as a parting gift. Apparently she really was a masochist because she couldn't stop wearing the darn thing. The single diamond was beautiful, elegant, and okay, it made her think of him. Which was good and bad. She shouldn't be thinking of him at all. She should be avoiding thinking of the stubborn, sexy man who'd stolen her heart.

"That's a seriously nice necklace." Nova's eyebrows rose a fraction. "And the man is a fool for walking away."

"Yes, he is," Layla said. "Because I'm awesome."

"That's what I like to hear. Are you sure you don't want company looking at this house?"

"Yeah, I'm sure. I've looked at almost a dozen so far. Once I figure out which one I want, I'll bring you. Until then, it's pretty boring."

"All right. I'm going to get out of here."

"I think I'm going to head out too. And I mean I'm going to head back to your place for good." She felt a little bad staying here at the ranch even though everyone had assured her it didn't matter. But Darcy and Brooks had been staying at one of his many condos downtown, and while it was a very nice one, she still wanted them to be able to come to their home freely. And she was tired of feeling like a nomad.

"You need help moving anything? I'm driving Gage's truck."

"I literally only brought a suitcase. Everything I own is still at your place so I'm good, but thanks for the offer." The only thing here other than her clothes was the snow globe Axel had picked up for her.

After more hugs, Layla grabbed her things and headed to her temporary home. She wanted to drop her stuff off and then meet her Realtor.

Maybe the thirteenth time would be the charm.

CHAPTER TWENTY-ONE

—Every end is a new beginning.—

L ayla pulled up to the ranch-style brick home, and scanned the front yard—which was huge—and realized she couldn't even see the neighbor's place because of the hedges on either side. That must be a thing in Redemption Harbor because they seemed to be everywhere. She liked all the greenery though. She didn't see her Realtor's hybrid Lexus SUV, but a BMW instead. Maybe the owners were home?

She parked behind it and texted Ellen. *Out front, where are you?*

Inside, checking out the space. It's gorgeous in person. Come take a look.

Be inside in a sec. Get a new car?

No, borrowing my husband's.

All right, then. She stepped out of her car, enjoying the feel of the warm sun on her face. It combated the icy cold in the air. Wrapping her scarf tighter around her neck, she shut her door and locked it.

When she saw the out of state plates on the BMW, she frowned. Ellen's husband lived in South Carolina too, she thought. Glancing inside the back window as she passed by, she was surprised by how immaculate it was. Ellen's vehicle was usually stuffed full of various yard signs, and her kid's car seat was missing.

Instead of heading in the front door, she rounded the back to check out the rest of the yard first. Mainly because the sun felt so amazing and she realized she'd been cooped up inside like a vampire for two weeks.

As she rounded the back of the house, her phone buzzed in her purse. Pulling it out, she froze when she saw Xavier's name on her caller ID. She'd told herself to delete his number. Had told him she was going to.

Well, she was a liar. She hadn't been able to take the very small step of simply removing him from her contact list. The move itself had seemed too final. And she wasn't ready to let him go yet.

She also wasn't ready to talk to him. What the hell was he doing? Dragging this out even longer? Despite the elation that surged through her at seeing his name, she silenced his call. She wanted to talk to him, desperately, and that was why she didn't answer. Her heart was racing out of control at the mere sight of his name and that was just a recipe for disaster. She was here to do something important to help get her life on track, and if she heard his sexy, rumbly voice, it would screw up her day.

Her heart was already broken. She couldn't deal with games or anything else. Not that she thought he was playing games...but she kinda wished he hadn't called. As she looked out at the backyard and pool area, something niggled at her mind.

The out of state license plate was pretty strange but now she remembered Ellen telling her that she and her husband were separated and about to get divorced. But she was driving his vehicle?

No...none of this felt right. Normally Layla and Ellen texted, but she knew from Nova that people could actually clone phones. What if...that had happened? And what if she was being crazy? But what if she wasn't?

That little alarm bell was going off in her head right now, telling her to leave. And she was going to listen to her instinct. She'd sworn to herself she'd never ignore her gut again.

As she hurried back around to the front of the house, she pulled her cell phone out of her purse. Maybe calling Xavier wasn't such a bad idea right now. She hoped she was just being paranoid but life had taught her to be aware.

At the front yard she saw that the trunk of the BMW was open and she could hear someone moving something around. *Shit, shit, shit.*

She couldn't get to her vehicle without passing the BMW. She froze, trying to decide what to do, then the trunk started to shut.

A man with dark, angry eyes stared at her for a long moment.

She didn't think. She turned and ran into the house.

The man cursed behind her.

Panic punched through Layla as she raced through the front door, looking blindly around as her fear ratcheted up.

She couldn't think. Could barely breathe as she vaulted upward, skipping steps on the set of stairs. As her legs carried her upward, she cursed herself. She should have run straight down the hallway and tried to find an exit door.

But her thoughts fractured as she tried to calm down and *think*.

Light spilled out from an open doorway. She raced inside and slammed it shut behind her, quickly turning the little lock. It was a bedroom.

Her phone started ringing again, the noise of it pushing through the haze of her mind. She swiped her thumb across the screen even as she raced for the nearest window. "Xavier, someone is after me," she rasped out.

"Layla!"

"No time," she panted, telling him the address as she reached the window. The phone tumbled from her fingers as she flipped the lock open.

She had to get out of here. And like a dumbass she hadn't stayed downstairs.

But she wasn't thinking, was barely functioning at this point. Never again would she judge people who made knee-jerk decisions at the height of panic.

Her fingers were practically numb as she struggled with the window.

Slam.

Slam.

Slam.

Oh God, he was kicking his way in.

She heard splintering wood as the frame cracked.

The window might as well have been nailed shut for all the strength it took her to wrench it upward.

As it finally broke free, icy wind blasted her in the face as the bedroom door crashed open, falling to the hardwood floor.

"Don't move!" The man stood there, his dark eyes angry, a gun in his hand.

He was pointing it directly at her.

She had a choice to make. Neither option was good. Take a chance with the man with the gun and hope he'd show mercy—which she knew he wouldn't. Or jump out the window and potentially break bones. And then get shot by this guy. These thoughts raced through her mind in milliseconds.

Screw it.

"No!" he shouted even as she rolled over the windowsill, praying for the best.

She cried out in pain as she landed in the cluster of thorny bushes, the sharp points tearing into her exposed cheek and ear.

Groaning, she scrambled to her feet, ignoring the additional slices of pain in her legs where the thorns had ripped through her jeans.

Run.

Find safety.

Get help.

She didn't glance back as dirt flew up next to her. Oh God, that asshole was shooting at her.

Her legs ached, her muscles straining as she ran around the side of the house and out of his line of sight. She needed to get to her car.

Sprinting, she nearly cried out again when she saw that her tires had been slashed.

She didn't pause, but continued running down the driveway, cursing how private this place was. But it was in a neighborhood at least. She just had to actually get to someone's house and hope they opened the damn door. Or at least she needed a place to hide because she didn't want anyone hurt because of her.

This guy had clearly picked this place perfectly.

And she'd walked straight into his trap.

* * *

Xavier's heart felt as if it would punch right through his chest as he gunned his engine. He'd almost had a heart attack when he'd heard Layla's terrified voice over the phone line.

Then those gunshots.

Fuck, the gunshots. Was she hurt? Had someone taken her? Or worse?

No. Not going there now. She had to be alive and he was going to get to her. Right fucking now.

He was so damn close too. Even before she'd told him the address, he'd already known where she was. Because he'd been using her phone to keep tabs on her the last two weeks. Like a fucking stalker.

Hard to feel any guilt now as he took a sharp left onto the street where her phone's signal was pinging from.

He should have claimed her weeks ago. He never should have walked away. He'd thought he was doing the right thing, but he hadn't even been able to leave Redemption Harbor. He hadn't been sleeping or eating.

Nope, he'd just spent all his time going over the information Gage had given him on the Murphy brothers—and obsessing over Layla. And he'd officially quit his job. He told his handler with the CIA he was done, and had rejected a few jobs and made it clear he wouldn't be taking any more. Ever.

He was done. Because he wanted Layla.

Now he might lose her forever because of his own stupidity.

As he tore down the driveway of the house he hoped she was at, he couldn't breathe for a moment as he saw her sprinting toward him, her eyes wide with panic.

Diego Gomez was running after her, a weapon in hand.

That son of a bitch. He was supposed to be dead.

Without thinking, moving purely on instinct, he rolled down his window. "Duck!" he shouted at the top of his lungs.

Half hanging out the window, pistol in hand, he was glad when she did exactly as he'd ordered. She dropped to the driveway as if her legs had given out.

He fired at Gomez. *Pop. Pop. Pop.*

Gomez cried out in pain as his body jerked backward. On the ground, Gomez kept firing even as he held a hand to a wounded shoulder.

Ping. Ping. Xavier's SUV shuddered to a halt, smoke billowing out of the engine as he threw open the driver's side door.

Without turning around he screamed, "Run!" He wanted Layla as far away from here as possible. Because even if he was killed, he wanted her safe. He wanted her to live. And if Gomez killed Xavier, he would have no reason to go after Layla anyway.

Sweet God in heaven, let her stay safe.

Adrenaline punching through him, he ran full speed at Gomez who was on the ground, pressing on his wound while still firing.

Xavier fired back, hitting him square in the middle of the forehead.

Even though he knew Gomez was dead, he continued the last few feet to the man's fallen body and checked his pulse.

Then he grabbed Gomez's pistol and tucked it in his waistband.

"Xavier!"

He turned to find Layla racing at him, her eyes wide with horror.

Xavier started toward her but his legs wouldn't obey him. He couldn't force his legs to move farther than three steps. What was wrong with him?

"Oh my God, oh my God, you've been shot!" She sounded as if she was in a tunnel. Everything sounded hollowed out as she shouted.

He'd been shot? That couldn't be right.

He looked down at himself, and realized that yeah, he'd taken a few rounds to the chest. He had on his tactical vest as usual but one of the rounds had hit just beyond the edge of the vest.

Ah, hell. He was going to pass out.

As darkness started creeping in at the edge of his vision, he was aware of Layla grabbing onto him and helping him to the ground.

"Where's your phone!" she shouted, her amber eyes sparking with raw fear.

"Pocket," he rasped out. His throat felt dry as he stared at her, pain starting to push into his consciousness. *Oh, fuck.*

"What's your code?" she shouted again, panic etched in every line of her beautiful face.

"Your birthday," he mumbled. His tongue felt too thick in his mouth right now and her face was starting to fade.

"Don't you fucking die on me! I love you, Xavier! Do not die! I won't let you!" Layla's shouted words rang in his ears as darkness completely swept him under.

She loves me.

CHAPTER TWENTY-TWO

—A scar means you survived.—

Xavier opened his eyes, disoriented as he looked around the huge bedroom. Plush sheets, lots of natural sunlight streaming in from bay windows. And a consistent *beep, beep, beep.* What the hell? Where was he? What...had happened?

Layla!

Oh God...relief punched through him when he saw her curled up directly next to him in a chair, a blanket pulled over her. Her long, dark hair was pulled up in a messy bun and her eyelashes fanned over her cheeks. Even in sleep, he could see dark circles under her eyes.

"Layla," he rasped out.

She jerked awake as if he'd fired a starter pistol, tossing the blanket off and letting it spill to the floor. "Xavier." She was at his side before he could blink, taking his hand between hers. She kissed the top of it over and over. "You're awake." Her voice was thick with unshed tears.

"You're okay?" He reached up with his free hand, his movements slow, to cup her injured cheek. About half a dozen small, angry-looking nicks covered her face.

"I'm fine," she said, tears spilling over her cheeks.

"My sweet Xavier," his abuela said, hurrying into the room.

"Wait...what are you doing here?" And where was here? He was hooked up to an EKG machine so clearly it was a medical facility of some sort. Though not like one he'd ever seen. It was too nice. Too quiet to be a hospital. But his left arm was in a sling, secured to his chest.

"Layla called me," his grandmother said, moving up behind Layla and patting her gently on the shoulder. "We are all here."

"Where is here?"

"In one wing of the Alexander Ranch mansion. Apparently being a billionaire means you have access to private doctors who don't call the police over gunshots," Layla said quietly.

His grandmother simply clucked her tongue and shook her head but there was no anger in her expression. Just worry. "We've been waiting for you to wake up. Layla hasn't left your side. Not even to shower so if you smell something, it's her," his grandmother said.

Layla gave a tired laugh as she glanced back at his grandmother. There was a wealth of love in her expression. In both their expressions. How long had he been out?

"How long..."

"A day. The longest day of my life. And let me tell you something," Layla snapped. "You are not going anywhere. You are staying in Redemption Harbor. And we are officially together. And you are quitting your stupid job."

"Yes, ma'am," he said solemnly. He loved Layla, and as soon as they were alone he was telling her. He remembered her screaming those words at him before he'd passed out, that she loved him. Even if she didn't, even if it had been in the heat of the moment, he knew what he felt and had to let her know.

She blinked once, as if surprised by his acquiescence. "All right then, as long as that's clear."

"I already quit. I couldn't leave Redemption Harbor anyway. It's why I was so close when... When everything happened. I was basically stalking you." His voice was raspy. He tried to swallow but his throat was too dry, making it difficult.

"Xavier," she said, gently stroking his arm. "Let me get you some water." She paused, looking at his grandmother.

His abuela pursed her lips. "He will be fine in the two minutes it takes you to get water. And call the doctor."

Nodding, Layla leaned over and kissed him quickly on the forehead before hurrying out of the room.

"You will marry that girl." His abuela's words were an order as soon as the door shut behind Layla.

"If she will have me."

"I'm sure she will. She's been sick with worry. Refused to leave that seat. And she only ate because I brought her food. And even then she barely touched it. I had to force her." Tears filled her eyes for the first time in as long as he could remember. "You better be serious about quitting your job," she rasped out. "We can't take the scare again. You cannot die before me."

"I'm really going to try not to die," he said, attempting to keep his tone light. But it was hard to talk when his throat was so dry. "Promise."

"Shush for now," she said. Then she pulled a little jewelry box out of her pants pocket. "Your grandfather gave me this when he proposed. You don't have to use it, but if you wanted to, I thought it would be nice for you to have something to propose with. Then you can pick out something later." She opened the little drawer of the side table and dropped it in there. "You know, when you ask that girl to marry you."

"Abuela..." He wanted to tell her it was way too soon, but Layla hurried back in with a man he didn't recognize who must be the doctor.

"Glad to see you're finally with us," the older man said, little lines crinkling around his eyes as he smiled gently at Xavier. "Ladies, I need to be alone with my patient."

"We're not going anywhere," Layla said, hands on hips as she stared at the doctor defiantly.

"Exactly what she said," his grandmother said, smiling much more sweetly than Layla, but her expression was no less defiant.

Sighing, the doctor shook his head and looked back at Xavier. "If these two ladies have their way, you're going to be on bed rest a lot longer than you need to be."

That was fine with him. Layla was alive. And so was he. Now he could finally pull his head out of his ass and claim the woman he loved.

As soon as he got out of this damn bed.

* * *

Layla trailed her fingers gently over Xavier's head before cupping his face. He loved the feel of her touching him and knew he'd never get enough of her hands on him. "I'm so glad you're awake."

"Me too." It was just the two of them now. After he'd talked to the doctor—and visited with his family—Layla had finally pushed everyone out of the room, claiming he needed rest.

Which wasn't far off from the truth. He was exhausted and in pain despite the meds he was on. But he wanted to stay awake now and talk to Layla. To get some answers to questions. Mainly, he just wanted to hold her hand, to know she was okay.

He was damn lucky that his vest had taken most of the bullets. According to the doctor, one missed and it had buried itself in the fleshy part of his pec. Oh, and he also had a fractured rib, which sucked. But the doc had dug the bullet out and was almost certain he was going to be okay. A small price to pay to have Layla alive and sitting right in front of him.

"I've got some blanks with what happened... I know I killed Gomez. But what happened to you? How did you get hurt?" He had too many questions and wasn't sure where to start.

"Well, to start with, he cloned my Realtor's phone. Ellen is fine, thankfully, and blissfully unaware of anything. He lured me to a house under the pretense that it was for sale. It's not for sale, but the owners were out of

town for a month in Florida. They talked about it on so-
cial media and that's how he found out—I only know this
because Gage ripped apart all of his electronics once they
found out where he'd been staying and that he was alive.
And, Nova's crew fixed everything in the house so that
it looks untouched. They also disposed of all vehicles...and Gomez's body." She shuddered slightly. "It's
weird to say that."

"The cops weren't involved?"

"No. No neighbors heard anything, given the time of
day."

"Good." That was one less thing to worry about.
"How did Gage miss Diego Gomez being alive?" To be
fair, Xavier had missed the guy too.

"He faked his death really well, apparently. That drug
runner really did try to kill him, so Gomez took advantage of it and faked his death. Gage told me a whole
lot of stuff in technical terms I barely remember. But the
gist of it is, since Gomez was presumed to be dead, Gage
didn't spend extra manpower trying to hunt him down.
And it turns out that Gomez is the one who turned over
our information to the Murphy brothers. Gage has an
electronic trail of it. Gage thinks he never planned for
the Murphy brothers to actually take you out—he thinks
those guys were too stupid. No, Gage thinks Gomez used
them to lure us out of hiding and into a false sense of
security. We'll never really know for sure. But he killed
the guy who hired you as well. He was going down the
line of anyone involved in the death of his brother and
the attempted kill on him."

That made a lot of sense. His head was starting to hurt, but he needed to know more. "Your face?" he asked, frowning as he lifted a hand to run a gentle thumb over one of her shallow cuts.

"Oh, right. I jumped out of a window to escape him and fell into a bunch of bushes. It could have been a whole lot worse and the doctor says I won't scar. Not that I even care about that." She cupped his face again, her expression filled with love as she looked at him. "I'm so glad you're alive," she whispered.

He covered her hands with his, looking into her bright eyes for a long moment. "I can't believe you stayed here the whole time." It humbled him that she'd stuck by his side. He'd done nothing but bring danger to her doorstep and here she was, holding on to him and looking at him as if he was the only thing that mattered. "I love you, Layla. More than anything."

She sucked in a breath. "I love you too. And I'm not going anywhere. And...I know what I said earlier," she said, sighing. "I didn't mean to order you around."

"It's okay. I like it when you're bossy. And I have quit that life."

"You were serious?" Hope flared in her eyes.

"Yes. I want a real life with you. I want a future with you and I want to see our kids grow up."

She blinked. "Kids? Do you know something I don't?"

He snorted softly, but stilled as a throb of pain pulled across his chest. He was damn lucky no major organs had been hit. But a fractured rib was going to be a pain in the ass. "I just mean I want the *chance* to have a future with you, and if you want kids, I want to have them with you. I'm not sure what kind of parent I'll be, but I know you'll be amazing."

To his horror, tears filled her eyes, but she swept them away quickly. "Don't say stuff like that."

"Why not? It's true."

She batted away more tears before leaning forward and kissing him gently. "We have plenty of time to talk about the future later. You just need to get better. If you don't, your grandmother and I will be on your ass anyway."

He grinned at the mention of his abuela. "You two seem to be getting along quite well."

"I really like her. She's feisty. She tried to tell me what to do when she first got here and I'm pretty sure I bared my teeth at her like a feral animal when she told me to leave your side. Honestly though, I think it was a test. And I must have passed because she's been nothing but kind to me since."

"You're most definitely right about it being a test. Hey, will you grab something in that side drawer for me?" He should probably wait to do something proper and more romantic but he'd almost died and couldn't go another second without claiming Layla forever. Hell, he would get a minister in here right now if possible.

Leaning over, she opened a drawer and pulled out the little jewelry box. "What is this?"

He took it from her delicate hands and opened it. "Layla Ferrer, will you marry me?"

She started crying again, but she nodded and it sounded like she said yes as he slid the ring onto her left hand ring finger. Then she was kissing his face, his cheeks, his forehead and then his mouth.

The door suddenly snapped open as they were kissing, his doctor and his grandmother striding in.

"Your heart rate spiked," the doctor said, looking between the two of them.

Layla held out her left hand for his grandmother, who grinned, her lined face filled with such joy he felt the warmth from his bed.

"Welcome to the family," she said, pulling Layla into a big hug.

"No getting Xavier excited," Dr. Safi said authoritatively. "He needs rest. Also, congratulations, you two."

Before Xavier could respond, a whole bunch of the Redemption Harbor crew came into the room.

The doctor looked exasperated but moved over to a corner of the room and started talking to Brooks in low tones as Axel came up to the bed. Nova was looking at Layla's ring, but she hadn't let go of his hand with her free one.

"I'm glad you're doing well," Axel said. "I also heard this was a wake-up call and you quit your job?"

He shifted against the soft sheets, exhaustion sweeping over him. "Yeah. And apparently Layla has lost her mind because she's agreed to marry me."

Axel squeezed him on his uninjured shoulder softly. "Congratulations, brother."

"Thanks."

It took less than two minutes for the doctor to shoo everyone out of the room. Everyone except Layla, of course. Because she wasn't going anywhere, and it was clear the man wasn't foolish enough to try to make her.

"I love you so much," he said to her as she sat back on the edge of the bed. "And I need to say this, so let me." He wanted to get all this out before he fell asleep and he knew that was coming sooner than later. "I'm sorry I pushed you away before. And I can't promise that there won't ever be any more danger for the two of us. But I'm going to do my best to insulate us from any future threat. And for the record, I might be a little crazy about your safety in the near future." Probably longer.

"That's fine with me. I love you and I want a long future with you. In fact, I'm pretty sure your family is moving up here now. Unless you want to move to Orlando?"

"I like it here." And he was pretty sure he'd be taking that job offer with Redemption Harbor Consulting. "I know my family will love it here too."

"Your cousins are having a ball riding horses with Valencia, so you're probably right about that."

"Good."

"Why don't you close your eyes for a little bit?" she murmured, sliding into the bed with him. This wasn't a standard hospital size so there was plenty of room. She curled up against him on his uninjured side, tucking herself where she belonged. Next to him. "I'm not going anywhere."

Feeling truly happy for the first time in forever, he did just that and closed his eyes. The woman he loved was by his side and wearing his engagement ring. As sleep played at the edge of his consciousness, he thought back to that night he'd met her and was grateful he'd seen Layla at his friend's rehearsal dinner. And he was doubly glad he'd had the balls to talk to her.

His life had been hollow before her, without any color, and she'd changed the landscape of his entire being. She was his everything now. And he was going to spend the rest of his life proving to her that she'd made the right choice with him.

EPILOGUE

—Live your adventure.—

"Looking good, Mrs. Stuart." Colt's voice was a sexy murmur as he slid up next to her.

Skye wrapped her arm around her husband's waist, laying her head on his shoulder as she looked out over their friends talking, laughing and dancing. Xavier and Layla's wedding ceremony was over and she was ready to slip off her heels. Unfortunately they were still at this shindig so she had to keep her shoes on. "Looking pretty good yourself." As always, her husband looked good enough to eat. But today more so because he was in a suit. Something he didn't always love.

But if she was wearing a dress—*a dress*—he was getting all fancy too. And the way it hugged his broad shoulders and chest was truly a work of art.

"Did you notice Layla isn't drinking?" His words were for her ears alone as they leaned against the built-in stone and brick bar on the outside patio of Brooks's huge backyard and pool area. The catering company had set up their own bar and weren't using this one. The murmur of everyone's voices rose and fell every now and then, the party still going strong.

This place had seen more than one wedding, including her own. "Yep. She's totally pregnant."

"What are you two gossiping about?" Nova sauntered over, champagne glass in hand, only slightly tipsy. She'd been helping Layla get ready for the wedding since this morning and Skye was pretty sure she hadn't eaten much.

"We don't gossip." Skye's tone was dry.

"Please. You're like two little old ladies over here. And I want in. What's up?"

"I was just telling Colt about the new Remington I got and—"

"Ugh. You're a liar but I'm not listening to gun talk. It's my best friend's wedding." She turned to look out over the small crowd of family and friends. "Though she's disappeared."

Skye snickered under her breath.

Nova turned back to look at her, eyes narrowed. "What?"

"Pretty sure she and Xavier snuck off somewhere to get naked. They'll be back later."

"But...they have to cut the cake." Nova stared at her in horror. "And she needs to throw the bouquet."

"Then go interrupt them," Skye said, grinning.

"Are you messing with me? Did they really sneak off?"

Skye just shrugged, fighting a smile as Nova hurried off, her heels clicking against the stone. Layla had said something about talking to the caterer and Xavier hadn't been willing to let her out of his sight for even two seconds, so he'd gone with her.

"You're mean." Colt buried his face against her neck, gently nipping at her skin.

Skye just laughed even as a shudder rolled through her. "Don't start, or you and I are going to sneak off for real."

"You say that like it's a bad thing." His breath was warm against her neck, but he pulled back just the same, his strong arm still around her. He'd recently gotten his hair cut so it was even shorter than normal—true military short. "What do you think of my dad's date?" He nodded once in the direction of Senior and the woman he'd been dating the last two months. Though today was the first time he'd introduced her to anyone.

"I like her. She thinks high heels are stupid and she gave me a tip on a new type of gun oil to try out." The woman was former Coast Guard and Skye's type of people.

Colt straightened, his green eyes surprised. "Seriously? When did you even have this conversation?"

"When you were busy stuffing your face full of appetizers."

"You mean filling up a plate for *you*?"

She shrugged, leaning in for a kiss. "I think he's found a winner with this one," she murmured. And she was glad that Colt and Senior had started to build a real relationship. Senior had helped out their crew on more than one occasion, and while he hadn't been the best father while Colt was growing up, he was here now. And he was trying. That had to count for something.

"Aunt Skye!" Valencia, Olivia and Savage's recently turned eight-year-old daughter raced at Skye and Colt, nearly running into Axel as she hurried over. Her frilly pink dress fluttered wildly, the ribbons in her hair doing the same as she practically launched herself into Skye's arms.

Skye caught her, laughing as she did. "Soon you're gonna be too big to hold."

Valencia grinned, revealing she'd lost another tooth. Man, this kid was the cutest. "Not today."

"Definitely not today." She kissed Valencia on the cheek. Over the last couple years Skye had gotten more used to showing affection, but it had come naturally with this one. It was pretty much impossible not to adore Valencia, one of the sweetest people she'd ever met. "Where're your mom and dad?"

"Talking to Mr. Alexander...and I wanted to show you something." She held up a slim diamond bracelet that had been on Skye's wrist earlier in the morning. "Did you notice it was gone?" she asked as Skye set her on the ground.

Grinning, Skye took the bracelet—she'd taught Valencia how to steal, much to Olivia's horror, but what was done was done. And the kid was damn good, and so cute she could probably get away with murder. "I didn't notice until about five minutes after you hugged me earlier." She held out the bracelet so Colt—who was shaking his head at the two of them—could fasten it. "You're getting better."

"I'm awesome!"

"Very true. But you're not stealing from anyone else, right?"

"Nope. Just you and Colt."

"Okay, good." Skye had been reamed out by Olivia when she'd discovered what Skye had been teaching her daughter, though Skye still didn't understand why she was mad. But she respected her friend, so as long as Valencia only practiced on Skye or Colt it was okay.

"I was grounded from riding horses for a week after last time. I'm not doing that again."

"Smart girl."

"Where's C-4?"

"At home, sleeping. I couldn't bring him to the wedding but I think you guys are coming over for dinner tomorrow, so you'll see him then."

"Okay, see you later." Like a whirlwind, she was off, running to catch up with one of her little friends.

"I bet you never thought you'd be here," Colt said.

"Where?"

"Here, surrounded by all these friends who we consider family."

"You're right, I never could have envisioned this." She never would have thought to, because once upon a time, something like this wouldn't have been her dream, let alone a possibility. Now it was. "But I'm glad we *are* here." Over the last couple years they'd created something real, something unbreakable. Something that would last.

She'd always felt like an outsider, a bit of a misfit—no wonder, considering she'd been raised by spies—and she'd always kept a very tight wall erected around herself. Until Colt.

He'd smashed that thing down and shown no quarter. And she was glad he hadn't.

Because now they'd truly created something great. They were helping people, and they'd built this wonderful life with people they loved. People who loved them back.

She looked over at Mary Grace and Mercer, standing by the pool. Mercer was holding his baby girl in one arm and had his other arm around his wife, looking as if he was holding a billion dollars in his hands. For a moment, she thought back to the day she'd met Mary Grace. She'd helped MG escape from a harrowing kidnapping situation in Mexico, and now here they all were, safe.

A team. A family.

Her throat tightened unexpectedly.

"Damn it, I think I might cry," she murmured. And that was unlike her.

"Don't worry, I won't tell." Colt held her close and kissed the top of her head as the DJ announced that it was time to cut the cake, a three-layer confection on a table near the dance floor.

Which made Skye perk right up. "Ooh, it's buttercream too."

Colt simply snorted. "Try not to knock over any little kids in your quest for food."

"No promises." When it came to food, she was a take-no-prisoners kind of woman.

It was impossible not to smile as she watched Xavier and Layla feed each other little pieces of cake, the love on their faces so evident. Just like the adoration of everyone watching—Lucy and Leighton, Savage and Olivia, Brooks and Darcy, who Skye was also pretty sure was pregnant, Axel and Hadley, Nova and Gage, and lastly Douglas and Martina.

Yep, this was worth holding on to. Worth protecting.

Just like the man she had her arm wrapped around. These were her people, her eclectic and crazypants family she adored.

She cuddled closer to Colt, a smile curving her lips. She was damn sure going to hold on to this man for the rest of her life.

Thank you for reading Chasing Vengeance. Writing this final chapter in the Redemption Harbor series was bittersweet. I'm sad to say goodbye to these wonderful characters but I felt it was time. If I ever get the urge, I'll revisit them again (maybe with a holiday story!). But for now, this is the end of this series. I hope you enjoyed it as much as I enjoyed bringing these characters to life. If you'd like to stay in touch with me and be the first to learn about new releases feel free to sign up for my newsletter at https://katiereus.com

ACKNOWLEDGMENTS

For my wonderful readers, thank you so much for sticking with this series and loving these characters as much as me. Your emails and messages online mean more than you know. For Kaylea Cross, once again I owe you a huge thanks for helping me plot this series and always being in my corner. And in no particular order I'm also incredibly grateful to Julia, Sarah and Jaycee. Thank you for helping me get this book ready for publication. And of course, I'm thankful for such a supportive family and to God for so many opportunities.

COMPLETE BOOKLIST

Red Stone Security Series
No One to Trust
Danger Next Door
Fatal Deception
Miami, Mistletoe & Murder
His to Protect
Breaking Her Rules
Protecting His Witness
Sinful Seduction
Under His Protection
Deadly Fallout
Sworn to Protect
Secret Obsession
Love Thy Enemy
Dangerous Protector
Lethal Game

Redemption Harbor Series
Resurrection
Savage Rising
Dangerous Witness
Innocent Target
Hunting Danger
Covert Games
Chasing Vengeance

ABOUT THE AUTHOR

Katie Reus is the *New York Times* and *USA Today* bestselling author of the Red Stone Security series, the Darkness series and the Deadly Ops series. She fell in love with romance at a young age thanks to books she pilfered from her mom's stash. Years later she loves reading romance almost as much as she loves writing it.

However, she didn't always know she wanted to be a writer. After changing majors many times, she finally graduated summa cum laude with a degree in psychology. Not long after that she discovered a new love. Writing. She now spends her days writing dark paranormal romance and sexy romantic suspense.

For more information on Katie please visit her website: www.katiereus.com

Made in the USA
Coppell, TX
24 August 2020